Paradise

Also by Janie Franz

The Bowdancer Saga

The Bowdancer

The Wayfarer's Road

Warrior Women

The Lost Song Trilogy

Verses

Refrain

Coda

The Premier

Sugar Magnolia

Ruins Discovery

Ruins Artifacts

Ruins Legacy

Handful of Dirt

Simple Gifts

Paradise

Janie Franz

Per Bastet

Paradise
Book 2 of the Granny Woman Tales

Copyright © 2025 Janie Franz

Published by Per Bastet Publications LLC, P.O. Box 3023 Corydon, IN 47112

Cover art by T. Lee Harris
ISBN 978-1-942166-92-4

Paradise

Chapter 1

Day 1: Monday, Dark Hollow, TN, afternoon

The old man raised the thermos mug to his lips. The ice-cold lemonade was most welcome after the trek down the mountain to the little cabin by the stream. He and his companion sat on the small porch, watching the changes in the light as the trees moved in a gentle breeze. "I can see why you like it here," he commented from a cane-bottomed chair.

"I'm sure there are such places on your land," the old woman said, sipping from a tin cup she had retrieved from the inside of the cabin. "Wish I'd brought some gin or Cousin Lije's brew. I'm aching."

Reaching into a small pack at his feet, the old man pulled out a tiny airplane-size bottle. He passed it to her. "Will vodka do?"

"Where'd you get that, Floyd Whiteman!"

"I picked it up at a convenience store on our way down."

"Must've not been a dry county then."

"I think it was back in Indianapolis." He twisted his body to inspect the porch ceiling and what he could see inside from the open cabin door. "This was a kit?"

"Yep. B.D. and his college friends built it."

"It might be easy to take apart." He cast her an inquiring look. "Unless you want to keep it here as a fishing cabin, a bonus to someone who might buy the land."

The old woman squirmed in her seat. "Well, this really isn't part of my land," she admitted. "It's in the National Forest. People here just sort of encroach, and it's kind of grandfathered in."

"Sephie, you're a squatter!"

She shrugged. "Family trait, I guess." Finishing her lemonade too quickly, she stood. "I don't know if I'll sell yet. But lord knows I can't keep going up and down that mountain, even if I ever decided to get a new hip."

"You need one?" Floyd asked, screwing the thermos mug back on the bottle and stuffing it into the canvas bag.

The old woman mumbled something.

"What was that?" he asked, straightening as he watched Sephie close and lock the door.

She faced him. "They said I've been needing one for a while. I just couldn't face letting my sister fuss over me. She always brought an edge to my tongue when I've been healthy."

"She won't be fussing over you now," he said, turning her toward the path up the mountain and lacing his arm through hers. "We'll bury her tomorrow."

"Lordy, Floyd. It will be an ordeal for your eyes."

He shrugged. "Every family has its own traditions. My people just mix the tribal with the Catholic service."

"I wonder if there's a parade of church ladies up top, waiting to gawk at me and offer me dishes of food that I really don't want to eat."

"You missing Bill's Lutheran funeral hot dish already?"

"Methodist," Sephie corrected. "His mother wasn't a Lutheran. But he put it on his menu as such."

"False advertising," Floyd said, chuckling.

"It sure was good."

"Want me to try to make some?"

"I doubt you'll find any kind of pasta in my kitchen. My people were potato Irish so no rice or pasta to be found anywhere. And my sister Agnesia wouldn't have known what to do with either."

"I can go to the store. Surely, they sell macaroni. Don't Southerners make mac and cheese?"

"Not my people."

"This will be a culture shock," he said.

Sephie laughed. "I'd never had fry bread or Indian tacos until I met you." She looked up at him. "I liked them."

"You were overcome by my charm," the old man said.

"I'm not 16," she said, paying attention to some tree fall in the path and carefully making her way over it with her companion's help.

"Is there some dish you really hope the church ladies bring?" Floyd asked.

"Well, I'd love a pot of green beans cooked the old-fashioned way or some greens and cornbread. And if one of them brought a blackberry cobbler, I'd be in heaven."

Re-looping her arm through his again, he said, "Let's see if heaven heard your prayers."

Chapter 2

Day 1: Monday, Freeman Funeral Home,
Dark Hollow, TN, evening

The Freeman Funeral Home was a massive old structure that once belonged to a Kentucky coal company owner. He'd chosen to slip over the state line to build this house because he didn't want any of his workers to see the opulence in which he was living. It hadn't worked since many of his workers had roots and relatives in East Tennessee. When the mine had closed and the company owner had left town, the gingerbread filigreed monstrosity was dedicated to the fate of many older, grander buildings in very small towns. It became the local funeral home. For these residents and their forebears, having that last ride in a Cadillac hearse and being laid out in grandeur was the ultimate way to get to heaven. It was the only way any of the dead or their relatives would ever see the inside of a Cadillac or such a stately mansion — unless they had a job cleaning or driving. And in Dark Hollow, no one could afford hiring out either.

As Floyd helped Sephie up the multitude of steps in front of the building, even he gawked at the sight.

"Impressive, isn't it?" Sephie said out of breath.

"More than I'd care to go out with."

"No big funeral homes up north?"

"Not on the rez. They're small, one-story affairs with just a big room or a yard where we mourners can gather. Not even in Bismarck. They're small, modern brick buildings. Efficient. Quiet."

"They used to bring them home for three days when I was young, and we'd all gather and eat and talk in front of the dead.

They did that with my grandmother," Sephie said, "back in the '50s."

"Makes sense," he said. "Not all this. . . " He waved his hand as they approached the big front door.

"I don't want all this," Sephie said. "Just bury me. Say a few words. And then have a big party and tell stories about me. The bigger and wilder the better. I won't be there to contradict you."

Floyd laughed, causing some people to turn their heads as they entered. He arranged his face into a more sober look as he released Sephie's arm and removed his black Stetson hat, twiddling with it between both hands. He didn't feel comfortable here, especially since he was the new man in Sephie's life. She'd been widowed for well over ten years and from what bits Sephie had told him, she hadn't entertained the idea much less the reality of having another man in her life. He was also a most imposing figure, his height and musculature from his bull riding days, and the fact that he was Mandan/Hidatsa. He owned his Mandan blood, but what was left had been diluted with that of the Hidatsa, his neighbors at the Three Affiliated Tribes at Fort Berthold Reservation in North Dakota, and that stray Welsh ancestor, who had gifted his family with a name that wasn't his but they could pronounce and remember: Whiteman.

As he stood among all these very White faces, he wasn't sure he'd be welcome or how deep prejudices ran here. When a half dozen women rose and rushed toward Sephie, he grabbed her left hand, uncertain if it was to reassure her or for her to steady him. To his relief, they mostly ignored him while Sephie endured hugs she didn't reciprocate and merely nodded at their outpouring of sympathy.

When Sephie swayed a little, Floyd took hold of her and the situation, guiding her to a chair. He sat down beside her, placing his hat on the empty chair next to him. Someone rushed to bring the old woman a glass of water, which occupied her attention for more time than was necessary to take just a few sips. The press of figures around Sephie caused Floyd to stand and gently say, "Ladies, please. She needs some room."

It was then that they eyed him critically like a bunch of laying hens, jerking their heads toward him, up and down and around, as if they'd found some fox invading their coop. He didn't miss their glance toward his left hand, looking for a ring, which wasn't there, and then toward Sephie's, which he still held in his hand, but they couldn't know for sure.

"Sisters," a short, round man chided gently. He had a military haircut and wore a black suit, white shirt, and black tie. Under one arm was a worn black Bible. "Let Sister Hill breathe."

Seeing Sephie's right hand tremble, Floyd rescued the glass of water.

"I'm Reverend Woods," the man said, extending his hand.

Floyd shook it, dropping Sephie's who slipped it under her right one. "Floyd Whiteman." Feeling awkward with the glass of water, he searched for a place to put it and set it on a low table that held a lamp and some tracts about heaven. He quickly returned to Sephie, sat down, and once more took her left hand into his. From what he could tell, she hadn't really responded much to Pastor Woods, except to nod at whatever he had said to her.

Finally, Sephie said to Floyd, "I want to see her."

The old man helped her up and took her to the casket. Almost lost in the white sateen lining, a wizened old woman lay with her shriveled hands folded at her waist. She was dressed in a black, cotton dress that looked as if it had been heavily starched and ironed, with only a small gold cross against the fabric. The dress looked as uncomfortable as the woman. The mortician had done little to enhance the woman's face, using hardly any color to produce a more lifelike appearance.

7

Floyd looked from the body to Sephie, trying to find a resemblance. There was only a faint one around the nose. It was hard to believe that the woman in the coffin was younger than the woman whose hand he held.

His companion reached toward her sister's folded hands. Briefly touching the back of her right hand to one of the dead woman's, Sephie's chin quivered, and then she quickly jerked her hand away.

Floyd offered her his folded white handkerchief, and she just covered her mouth with it. When she turned, he guided her back to their chairs.

Taking a shuddering breath as she sat, Sephie said to him. "I can't do this."

"Let's leave then."

She shook her head. "No. We have to stay for all of it."

"All of it?" he questioned.

She raised her eyes to his. "Just be my strength."

Having no clue what to expect, Floyd just put his right arm around her and still held her hand with his free one.

Sephie offered him a small smile. "You'll raise eyebrows." But she didn't tell him to remove his arm.

"I already have," he admitted.

And so, they sat for three solid hours, as church members came and left, offering their condolences. Sephie emerged from her initial grief after the first half hour and was able to make sense of the people, who spoke to her, each telling her about a quality that her sister Agnesia had or some small story about her cooking or sewing skills she had offered to the church at various functions. The final half hour was a prayer service that Pastor Woods led that only offered one hymn, "Amazing Grace." Floyd could have endured the tedium of the funeral visitation if there had been music and food and some laughter as stories were told like he would have experienced in his hometown. This was austere and hard, making mourning even more difficult.

8

When he finally got into the truck, Floyd asked, "How are you holding up?"

"Lord, I need a drink," the old woman beside him said, resting her head against the seat back.

Floyd laughed and started out of town. "I might join you."

"You don't drink."

"If I had to live like that every day, I'd start."

"I think that's why all of the menfolk in my family of my father's generation were all moonshiners."

"Don't you have a cousin who's still making it? Isn't that where all those Mason jars of 'shine came from that you brought to Mandy and Laura's shop up North?"

"Well, yes, but it's not for drinking. You know that. It's for my tinctures."

Floyd smiled, seeing the feisty Sephie back that he'd come to know. "I think we'd both benefit from some food. I thought these things had groaning tables of food."

"Not the visitation in a funeral home. If I'd been here when Agnesia died, that lot would have been camping in my living room for three days before now. But I think the church ladies feel they've done their duty with the food they brought today. I doubt if there'll be a lunch after the funeral."

"You didn't seem to like anything they brought."

"If I see another pan of banana pudding, I'll scream!"

"Four pans were excessive."

"And it won't keep. I've never been fond of it, and Agnesia never made it, thankfully. She never made desserts." She was silent a moment. "Her biscuits were good though."

"Think anything's open in town?" Floyd asked.

"Lord no! This town closes up everything at 8 o'clock."

"How about the next town?"

She sighed. "I guess we can go home and fry eggs."

"You were looking forward to a pot of green beans."

Sephie suddenly burst into tears.

9

All Floyd could do was put his hand on her knee and steer the truck toward Sephie's mountain home.

Chapter 3

The old woman padded into the bedroom in her bare feet, heading to her closet for the sensible low heels she'd put on her swollen feet that matched her black funeral dress. It was a given that she'd have such a dress, living with her sister because Agnesia had dragged her to every funeral that little Primitive Baptist Church had. Sephie always wondered if it was Agnesia's way to offer an object lesson for her sister's sinful ways, a reminder that she needed to get right with God. Sephie never considered herself a sinner, especially. Sure, she nipped a little gin down at her cabin, but it was medicinal, though she did enjoy it. And she danced once in a while when she was married. She never swore much, and she dressed comfortably but modestly. Sephie always wondered what kind of sinning she was supposed to be doing and whether she was missing out on some fun.

Finding her shoes, she sat on the edge of the bed and put them on as Floyd entered, fingering the French cuffs of his black shirt. "That's a handsome shirt," Sephie said.

"I don't suppose I can roll these up for the funeral like I do back home when I direct the choir."

Sephie crossed the room to examine the cuffs. "I got just the thing." She moved to a high dresser and pulled a wooden jewelry box toward her. Floyd followed her. She opened the lid and rummaged inside, pulling out a pair of silver cuff links. Etched in each was a tree with wide branches. She handed them to Floyd.

"Your husband's?" he asked. But didn't allow her to answer, offering them back to her. "I can't wear these."

Sephie pushed them back into his hand. "Yes, you can. They were a door prize at a business Christmas party. My husband hated them, saying they were tacky, and never wore them." She gazed at them now. "I always liked those." Looking up at him, she added, "They suit you. They're yours."

Floyd looked at the delicate work. "Thank you," he said and put them into his cuffs.

"Do you have a tie to go with that shirt?" Sephie asked.

"Is it required?"

"What do you wear back home in church?"

"I wear a suit but no tie. I just wear the cross one of my nephews carved for me. It ties me to my tradition."

Sephie touched his arms with both hands. "Then that's what you should wear today if you brought it."

"I always have it," he said. Reaching into the jewelry box for something he noticed, he pulled out a simple gold wedding band. "Yours?"

She nodded.

Floyd reached for her left hand, but she pulled it away.

"What are you doing?" she demanded.

"I want you to wear this today. I saw enough snooty looks from those church ladies last night. They kept trying to see if you had on a ring."

"Is that why you kept holding my hand? So they wouldn't see?"

He nodded. "I'm a stranger and native. They've seen that I'm staying in your house. I'm sharing your bed, though that's been innocent enough. They don't need to know you've hardly known me a month. The whole town may come out to this funeral if last night's visitation was any indication. So, please wear this today."

Sephie frowned, pressing her lips together in disapproval. Finally, she just nodded.

Floyd slipped the ring onto the proper finger of her left hand. "When the time is right, this will be done in the way of my people."

She blinked. "Did you just propose?" she asked softly.

"I thought I already had."

Sephie remembered him urging her not to make this trip from North Dakota alone. In the stillness of the kitchen of the little house, next door to the North Star, her grandniece's metaphysical shop, he had asked her to "give us a chance" right after she'd gotten the news about her sister's passing. She hadn't really said "yes," but she hadn't said "no" either. And in her heart, she knew her answer. Now, after spending every minute with him for several days, she was sure. "I don't recall saying 'yes,'" she teased him. She watched his eyebrows lift in surprise and then slowly fall in defeat. She couldn't bear his disappointment so she added, "Ask me again sometime."

She started to move away when Floyd stopped to kiss her. This time she pulled him closer and kissed him back. When she stepped away, she saw an astonished look on his face.

"That was a 'yes,'" he said.

She pursed her lips together to hide her smile and headed for the closet again to find the little black funeral hat with the veil.

Chapter 4

Day 2: Tuesday, Church in the Valley,
outside Dark Hollow, TN, midmorning

The truck rolled onto the gravel driveway that led farther into a wood of pine and oaks that abutted the national forest. Almost a mile in, a plain church building stood, faced with white siding and sporting a thin, stingy line of black trim around the windows and the double doors of the building. Above that entrance was a white sign, painted in black letters: Church in the Valley. Farther into the trees, gravestones sprouted like remnants of ancient crops. Nearby, a blue canopy had been secured over several folding chairs set up on a patch of artificial turf. Beside it was an open maw. The orange clay soil from it had been mounded to the far side. Another patch of artificial turf tried to cover it, but not completely, as if everyone was ashamed of raw nature.

Sephie watched Floyd switch off the truck engine and frown at the graveyard while he unbuckled his seatbelt. She worried how he would react to this very different deep-water Baptist service. Catholic funerals were dignified and had a particular order that everyone knew. She herself didn't know what to expect since she didn't attend services here like her sister did. Each funeral she had attended though was different here, suited to the person who had died. All she knew about today was that whatever happened would be for effect and really would have little bearing on her own grief. She sighed and followed Floyd's lead by unbuckling her own seatbelt.

His phone rang in the silence, intruding into her thoughts and possibly his. Reaching into his shirt pocket, he checked the ID and brightened. "Yolanda, how are you, and how's the baby? Did you think of a name yet?" He listened and chuckled. "It'll get easier. Did Wes get in?" This time as he listened, his face grew serious until he was frowning. "Of course, you can. It's your house." He cleared his throat. "When do you think you'll head out?" He nodded to no one as if Yolanda could see his approval. "I understand. Just leave the address with Mandy and Laura when you go. I love you, Granddaughter." He ended the call. Still holding the phone in his left hand, he leaned his arm on the car window as he covered his mouth with the back of his hand.

"What is it?" Sephie asked gently.

Floyd just shook his head, shoved his phone in his pocket, and reached to pull his key from the ignition.

"Now, don't you go all Indian on me, old man," Sephie accused.

His face looked incredulous. "What did you say?"

"You know. Retreat into stereotypical stoicism. You're hurting about something. Are Yolanda and the baby all right?"

"They're fine," he said. "They named the baby Mara after Mandy and Laura. Sort of smooshed the names together."

He pulled his phone out of his pocket again and fidgeted with it. "You should turn your phone off or put it on vibrate."

Harrumphing, she fished her phone out of her handbag and turned the sound off. When that was done, she dropped it back inside, purposely letting the clasp ring out loudly. "And?" she prompted.

He swallowed. "Wes' parents brought him from the airport, and they're going to take Yoland and Mara back to Wisconsin with them. Wes only has a couple of days off so he'll go to my house with all of them and pick up Yolanda's things and all of the baby furniture. They rented a small U-haul trailer for the trip." He turned to Sephie. "She called to ask permission for them to enter my house and move her things. Permission?"

He looked away.

Sephie touched his arm. "It was proper to ask."

"But it's her home. It has been for most of her life."

Sephie gently rubbed the crisp sleeve of his shirt. "You can go visit her, Floyd."

Facing her once more, he said, "She won't know who she is."

"You mean Mara?"

"Yes, and Yolanda will forget."

"You'll bring your people to them when you visit just by being you." She patted his arm. "And you'll think of ways to fill the empty rooms." The old woman smiled and eased herself closer to the door to open it. She slid out as she always did and closed the door, crossing behind the long truck bed to meet Floyd as he locked his door. In the soft morning light, she approved of his black shirt with the silver tree cuff links, the carved wooden cross hanging from a thin strip of black leather, his dark pants held up by his belt with the silver rodeo buckle. He'd never showed her that before.

"You look very handsome today," she said.

Floyd wrapped her arm through his and patted her hand. He clinched his jaw as if he said anything more, he'd reveal emotion in front of the people that were flowing into the church building.

Sephie gripped the old man's arm, arming herself against the onslaught of pitying looks that also sought out something to gossip about. Inside, they made their way down the aisle past rows of polished, blonde-stained, wooden pews toward an empty one up front that awaited them. At the end of the aisle, the casket sat on a metal gurney that was blocked from view by large baskets of flowers. There were more flowers set up on either side and on the riser behind where the pulpit overlooked the coffin. On the far right was a brown leather armchair and on the far left was another one. Behind the pulpit, eight chairs were filled by four men and four women, each with a hymnal in red library binding. There was no piano or organ or any other instruments to be found.

When Floyd stopped at the first pew, Sephie said, "We have to look at her again."

He led her to the open casket, which now bore two small containers of flowers, propped against each far corner.

"Goodbye, sister," Sephie said. "I hope heaven is all you hoped it would be."

"May her journey be swift," Floyd said.

"Amen," the old woman said and turned toward the empty pew.

With a hand on her elbow, Floyd guided her into the seat, where she sat down wearily. Taking his place beside her, he noticed the red hymnals in a narrow shelf in front of him. He flipped through them, only recognizing a few of the titles.

"B.D. would enjoy the singing," Sephie said softly.

"Yes, he would," Floyd said, looking up. "I don't see any instruments. No piano. Is there an organ somewhere?"

"No. Primitive Baptists don't approve of music, only singing."

He nodded, putting the hymnal back in its place.

"Brother Whiteman," Pastor Woods said from the aisle and then came around to the front of the pew to extend his hand. "So good to see you here this morning."

Floyd shook his hand. "It's a sad day."

"But our dear sister is now in Glory. We can celebrate that." He turned to Sephie and reached both of his hands toward her. "Sister—" He began but stopped as he saw the wedding ring on the old woman's left hand. "Sister Whiteman," he said, evident relief in his voice. "God is with you during this time. We just need to look up and know your dear sister is looking down on us all."

"Thank you," Sephie muttered, gently pulling her hand away from his.

"Brother Whiteman, since you are family now, we'd like you to be a pallbearer. One of our members has graciously stepped aside for you."

Surprised, Floyd looked at Sephie who just nodded. "I'd be honored," he said.

"The funeral directors will move the casket to the front door. You and the others will carry her to graveside." He turned to Sephie. "The church ladies will take care of you."

Sephie gasped and then searched in her purse for her handkerchief to cover her mouth.

"God bless you, sister," Pastor Woods said and took his place behind the pulpit.

Floyd put his arm around Sephie's shoulders. "You ok?"

She muttered as the choir stood, "Lord save me from those women."

The eight voices began with "Shall We Gather at the River," which prompted the entire congregation to rise and find the hymn in the hymnal.

Sephie and Floyd remained seated. After looking at the index, he found the hymn and what verse they were on and joined in. At another service, Sephie would've sung, but she just couldn't. She listened to the harmonies the country choir and the congregation produced and even bent her head to smile at Floyd's rich voice. She also saw how quickly the church embraced the old man once they thought she and Floyd were legally married. There was something disturbing about all of it. She also wondered if tongues would be wagging later this afternoon because he wore so much bling and not a wedding ring himself. Primitive Baptists only approved of wedding bands for their members and no other jewelry; although a woman could get away with wearing an engagement ring as well as a band. Men often chose not to wear a ring, though. Floyd had looked so handsome that morning she didn't care. He was being accepted in a small way. She was sure, however, she'd never set foot in that church again so it shouldn't have really mattered, but it did somehow.

Chapter 5

Day 2: Tuesday, Church in the Valley,
outside Dark Hollow, TN. near noon

Outside the double front doors of the church, Floyd and five other men hoisted the highly polished oak coffin onto their shoulders. From his place in the rear of the group, he was surprised that the weight he bore was so little and wondered why they needed six pallbearers. Then remembering the frail body he'd seen in the box, he guessed the old woman hadn't weighed more than a hundred pounds.

Actually, moving the body to the gravesite was the only practical thing to do since the loose gravel would have made travel with the gurney difficult. Back home, Floyd had carried family members to gravesites before, but that had been over hard packed earth, dotted with scrub. This was tricky but not impossible. His position in the back made it easy for him to steady their communal burden if someone stumbled. Floyd's only worry was Sephie being surrounded by all of those clucking church ladies.

By the time the pallbearers had placed the casket onto a metal mechanism that would lower it into the ground, the rest of the congregation had already gathered inside and around the canopy. Floyd turned to find Sephie in a chair facing him. She was being fussed over by four ladies of the church, who were relating their affections for Agnesia. Floyd stepped to her rescue to take his place on a chair beside her. Other women of the church sniffed as they placed all of the flowers from the church around and over the closed coffin; they touched delicate handkerchiefs, edged in white cotton crochet thread, to their eyes.

One of them wailed like a paid mourner in some Eastern European country and draped herself across the polished wood. "You will be so missed, Sister! We loved you so much!"

Another wailed, "You selflessly served the Lord's church." And she dropped down on her knees in front of the casket. "You were an example for us all."

And someone else, behind Floyd and Sephie blurted out, "We'll never replace your chicken and dumplings!"

While someone else said, "Or your green beans! You blessed the church with your canning."

And another called out, "You served the Lord selflessly!" and began to wail even louder than the woman still sobbing over the casket.

"You were the best chicken fryer among us!" Another woman yelled out.

Floyd had to press his lips together tightly while bowing his head to keep from emitting a guffaw. From the corner of his eye, he saw Sephie cover her mouth with her handkerchief, her shoulders shaking. He was certain it wasn't from crying. Whether to offer comfort or appreciation of her good sense, he put his arm around her shoulders.

Sitting in the breeze under the canopy, Floyd appreciated being outdoors. It had been a long morning in a church without air conditioning, making him glad he hadn't brought his suit.

Floyd had enjoyed the singing during the service. What the pastor said about Sephie's sister was touching since the Reverend did seem to know the woman well. That wasn't always the case at all funerals. A couple of the elders in the church — men — told stories that their wives had told them about Agnesia's dedication to the Sewing Circle and how she had helped cook food for the shut-ins of the church for years. But no women spoke there but were vocal outside. The prayers were equally heartfelt and long. Finally, the pastor had ended the service before the last hymn with a plea for sinners to come to the altar for forgiveness. Floyd found that quite odd and inappropriate. However, he figured these people would find Catholic masses or his tribal gatherings equally foreign.

The old man was becoming thirsty and hungry. He wondered if there would be a big dinner in the church, but he hadn't seen a separate hall in the building that would house events like that. The church was so small and seemed to only have the sanctuary with a small hallway that had led to an office and a bathroom.

Looking over at Sephie, who was slumped against him, he saw her evident weariness. She had hardly spoken since entering the church as if the very life had been sucked out of her, but it may have just been the restrictions placed on women. He remembered that even at the visitation the night before, she had been subdued. Now, it was evident she needed food and drink much more than he did. Floyd wondered if these long funeral events were somehow a test or a penance. This funeral today was well into its third hour, just as last night's visitation.

He glanced down at Sephie's feet crammed into her dress shoes. Her ankles were swollen. It reminded him of Yolanda's brush with pre-eclampsia a few weeks before and that brought him back to his own grief of missing his granddaughter and her new baby because they were moving. There was nothing to draw him back immediately to his house on the Fort Berthold Reservation in North Dakota. But he didn't want Sephie to have to linger here longer than she had to, lest the visits by the church ladies loosen her very colorful tongue at their attempts to pray her into heaven as her sister had tried to do for years.

Floyd pulled her even closer against him. She needed his stability and, in some ways, he needed hers. They sat listening to "Precious Lord" and "I'll Meet You in the Morning," and the cadence of Pastor Woods as he prayed for Agnesia and Sephie. While the breeze washed over them both, Floyd enjoyed the peace in that moment and pressed his cheek against Sephie's temple. Unexpectedly, she squeezed his thigh against hers, causing him to bend his head toward her as she looked up at him. In her eyes was a silent plea.

Immediately after the last "Amen," he rose, helping Sephie to her feet. He noticed that she took more time than usual to get her body settled over her shoes after she had been sitting for a long while. He assumed it was her swollen ankles and maybe her feet as well. Putting his arm around her and holding onto the arm closest to him, he guided her away from the gravesite, even as people crowded toward them. Acting like a slow-moving quarterback navigating through the church members, he maneuvered Sephie around them, offering only a "Thank you" or an "Excuse me" as he passed.

At his truck, he gave Sephie more help climbing into the vehicle than he normally did with no complaint from her. Her face was covered with perspiration as he fastened the seatbelt around her. As soon as he could, he kicked on the air conditioning and barreled down the long, gravel driveway to the blacktop that led to Dark Hollow. Ignoring the speed limit, he raced into town to a hamburger place he thought he remembered was there and finally pulled up to the drive-through window.

He looked over at Sephie to ask what she wanted. Her eyes were closed as she leaned back against the seat. He ordered Cokes, cheeseburgers, and a big order of fries. Grateful that it didn't take long to get an iced drink in his hand, he passed it to Sephie. She didn't rouse even when he called her name. Gently, he touched the cold paper container against her hand, and she moved.

"Drink," he urged.

Clumsily, she took the soft drink into both of her hands, but Floyd kept his hold on it to keep it steady. He pulled the container away and put it into a cup holder that rested over the hump that ran the length of the vehicle. "Pace yourself," he said, before taking a drink from his own soft drink.

Fries came next, and Floyd offered those to her. When she took the bag of fries, he touched the back of his hand to her forehead. It was cool but still moist.

By the time the cheeseburgers appeared at the window, Sephie had revived somewhat. The saltiness and the cold drink restored some fluids and sodium to her body.

Floyd turned the truck back onto the highway and headed out of town in the opposite direction from which they came. "Feeling better?" he asked.

She nodded, then took a bite of the burger. As she chewed, she rewrapped it and put it on the bench seat beside them before reaching for his that he'd placed next to his leg.

He glanced down at her actions. "You that hungry?"

She just unwrapped a portion of the burger, leaving the paper secure over the bottom and handed it to him. Then, she took two napkins and tucked them into his shirtfront. "Too nice of a shirt to drip on," she said.

He smiled. "You really like this shirt, don't you?"

Returning to her cheeseburger, she said between munches, "I might want to go on a date with that shirt, old man."

He chuckled. "You are feeling better."

She swallowed and reached for her soft drink. "Not that better."

Chapter 6

Day 2: Tuesday, Sephie's home,
Dark Hollow, TN, late afternoon

Stretched out on a chaise lounge on the front porch that was in full shade from the afternoon sun, Sephie sipped a red icy concoction from a tall glass. "What is this again?"

"Watermelon Agua Fresca."

"It's wonderful! Do your people make it?"

"No. Patricia's family serves it at their taco restaurant."

"So, you got her to tell you her recipe on one of your Summer Solstice trips to Riverbend?"

"Your great-niece had some, and it looked interesting. If you like watermelon, you'll probably like it. I did add some salt because you needed it. I think you got overheated and dehydrated today."

"I always put salt on my watermelon," she said and took another drink. "This is addicting."

Floyd slid his long frame into another chaise and sipped from his own glass.

"I'd give up liquor in my lemonade for this," she said.

"I may save your soul yet," he teased.

She twisted her head toward him. "You thinking of taking over Agnesia's job?"

"No," he said seriously. "Nothing wrong with a drink now and then. There comes a time, though, when liquor just can't ease the pain in the bones . . . or the heart."

"Amen to that. I wished I'd taken ibuprofen with me today."

"There wasn't even water to take it with. How do those

people manage services without air conditioning and something to drink in this humidity?"

Sephie sighed. "They're a hard people. They enjoy suffering for the Lord."

"I wondered about that. It was a long service."

"Well, I'm not setting foot in that place again. It did today for my sister." She then said, "I appreciate your tolerance."

"I'm all for ecumenism," he said, drinking more of the watermelon drink.

"You got any questions?"

He was silent for a moment. Then he said, "No women spoke in church. Is that common?"

"Women are vocal behind the scenes as you saw with all that drama around the casket. I was surprised they hadn't done that at the visitation." She eyed him again. "I think they were suspicious of you."

Floyd harrumphed.

"But, no, women aren't permitted to preach or lead prayer. They can sing, and they can make a prayer request if they ask a man to bring it to the church during the service."

"And that's a Baptist requirement?"

"No, it's a requirement of this particular primitive Baptist congregation. What you don't understand is that fundamentalist denominations will split and break off into other denominations over the most trivial things. The ministers aren't formally trained. They just have to be called by God, and some aren't even properly ordained. In some churches, they would only be anointed evangelists. But the congregations could oust a preacher as quick as snapping your fingers. And they did once. Before Pastor Woods. The preacher's wife ran off with another man. The church pronounced judgment and the preacher was turned out."

"Whatever for? He didn't do anything wrong."

"They said if he couldn't control his wife, how could he possibly lead a congregation."

"Good lord! And your sister approved?"

"It was her life. Always has been."

"But not yours?"

"You pegged me from the beginning. I was raised in this, but my husband was a Southern Baptist, more progressive as far as Baptists go. But I'm a maverick. I reach back into the older ways of my ancestors like you do. It's found in the land not in a building or a book."

Floyd sat up to put his drink on a little glass table between them. "So, you'll stay on this land then?"

"I—" she began. "I don't know. I am drawn here to these woods I've known since I was able to scramble in them as a child. But I saw the mountains taken over by the coal companies and now the developers. Progress will ruin what I loved here whether I stay or sell or leave it to my daughter and her husband. This will all become mountain condos or resorts."

"Ouch," he said.

"It's a reality." She sighed again. "If I leave it to my daughter, it will only delay it maybe a year or two until they decide how they'll profit by developing it or selling it themselves. If I sell, it will be immediate." She put her glass down on the table. "I just don't want to see it when it happens."

Pushing his leg over the side of the chaise, Floyd sat up, folding his hands in front of him. "I understand the tie to a specific piece of land and the spirituality that holds, ties to ancestors and the Creator and the spirits of the land itself." He looked down as if gathering his thoughts. When he looked up, he added, "It's different with every piece of land, but all land has it. Spirituality is a function of place. You can find spirituality in other land if you take the time to seek it out."

She studied his serious face. "You trying to sell me on North Dakota? Or on you?"

He tilted his head. "Would it be so bad?"

"Honestly," she answered, avoiding the relationship question, "I haven't really seen much of that state."

"Then let me show you." He reached out to take her hand.

"Would you teach me about the spirits of the land?"

He smiled. "They will teach you themselves."

"And there're medicine plants there?"

"Just like here. Some alike. Some different. Some I don't know, but I know people who do." He smiled again. "There are stories in the land. Stories about my people. About the plants. About the seasons. Different, yes. But Spirit is there."

Floyd's phone rang, and so did Sephie's.

"That sure broke a mood," the old woman muttered, reaching for her phone.

Floyd raised an eyebrow at his caller ID and stepped farther down the porch.

Thinking it was Mandy, Sephie didn't bother checking the ID. "I'm fine, Mandy. You don't need to be such a mother hen. I've seen far too many old biddies today anyway."

The girlish giggle and the gurgle of a baby in the old woman's ear signaled that it wasn't her great-niece. "Oh, I'm sorry."

"It's all right, Miss Sephie," Yolanda said. "I just wanted to check on you and how you were after the funeral. It sounds like you're fine."

"It's been a long couple of days. And the church house was way too hot."

"Wasn't the air conditioning working?

"They don't believe in it. They just open the windows and turn on a few fans. But the church was crowded."

"They must have really loved your sister."

"Or they wanted to take a look at the new man her wayward sister brought and hoped they were married." She chuckled. "Your grandfather made me wear my old wedding ring just so there wouldn't be any gossip."

"Has he officially proposed yet?"

Sephie heard the excitement in her voice as she had often

heard in Laura's and Mandy's sometimes when they teased her about Floyd. "No, but I think he's getting close. He thinks he has twice before though."

She laughed. "Put him out of his misery, Miss Sephie. Say 'Yes.'"

"In due time, little miss. How's the baby?"

"Adjusting very well since we have been hither and yon since the day she was born." She paused. "How's Grandfather? Really? I know he must've taken our moving really hard."

"It hurt. But he's coping. You have to do what's best for the baby. And you're really a city girl anyway."

"Well, at least a townie."

"You need family around you to help with Mara since Wes is away so much flying."

The baby started to fret and someone took her out of earshot. "I'm really glad Grandfather has you. You match his stubbornness. You won't let him get away with worrying about me."

"We'll visit soon."

"Are you staying there or coming back here?"

"We're negotiating that now."

"Ooooh. Negotiating before the proposal."

"You have to come back if there's a wedding."

"Grandfather will want all the ceremonial and legal trimmings. He never got that with Grandmother. They were married by a justice of the peace."

"We'll see, my dear. Kiss the baby for me."

As she said goodbye, Floyd returned to his chaise. "That wasn't Mandy on your line because she called me."

"It was Yolanda. What did Mandy want? Are she and Laura and B.D. all right?"

"They're fine." He shook his head at his phone and put it on the glass table. "Checking up on us, right?"

Sephie nodded. "We got good kids in our families. I think none of them thought we'd tell them the truth."

"We wouldn't." Floyd laughed and reached for Sephie's hands again. "Sell or leave your home to your daughter. That's not important to me." Then, he looked embarrassed. "I'd get down on one knee, but I think you're too weary to help me get back up, and I don't think I can do it by myself." Then he said soberly. "Sephronia Hill, will you be my wife?"

She pursed her lips to hide her smile and then couldn't. She grinned back at him as she eased her body upright and swung her legs to the side of the chaise. "Floyd Whiteman, yes, I will. But, let's do the ceremony in North Dakota on your land among your people. We'll plan it right, and bring Yolanda and Mara back for it." She paused. "I've decided. I'm going to sell. My daughter and her husband have plenty. I could use some ease in my old age, and the money will help us both." She leaned closer to him. "And we can continue to live in sin until it's legal. I don't really think anyone cares."

Instead of grabbing her and kissing her, he bent over the hands he held and touched them to his lips. When he raised his head, his eyes were glistening with tears.

Sephie was so moved she flung her arms around him and kissed him from her heart, oblivious to the fact that both of them were way too weary to follow where that would lead.

Chapter 7

Day 3: Wednesday, Sephie's home,
Dark Hollow, TN, morning

Coming down the narrow stairs for yet another time, Sephie grimaced at the ache in her hip. If she thought going up and down the mountain had become nearly unbearable for her, the old stairs were soon going to be as impassable as those ridges and hollows outside of her door. She took a deep breath or two so she could arrange a more pleasant expression on her face before she followed the smell of spicy country sausage and eggs frying in an iron skillet into the kitchen.

"Well, now," she said. "I could get used to this."

As he had done for many mornings in Riverbend and now here in her home, Floyd was putting a hearty breakfast together. He turned to smile at her. His face was now framed in two long braids tied with rawhide. The old man poured her a mug of coffee, and then stepped to her, pausing to put his arm around her waist, pull her close, and kiss her longer than a good morning peck.

Sephie was surprised. But the old man had always been unpredictable. When she pulled away, she merely said, "You're gonna burn your sausage, old man."

He chuckled. "Oh, you think I will?" he teased, adding another meaning to her simple caution about the food on the stove. "You seemed to keep up pretty well last night."

She backhanded his chest and took the coffee mug from him. Sipping it, she said, "You don't have to keep making the coffee so weak. I can always water it down."

Turning back to the stove, he took his pans off the burners

and dished up two plates. "It's a little change. It's probably better for me."

"You should've woke me up earlier. I'd've made biscuits."

"No worries. I made Texas toast."

Opening the oven door, he pulled out a baking sheet with four slices of pre-buttered toast.

Sephie brought the plates to the table and sat down. When Floyd joined her, she offered a brief blessing over their food and picked up her fork to find Floyd smiling at her. "What?" she asked.

"I never get tired of hearing you pray."

"Well, it's a pitiful little grace. Agnesia could bring chills down your spine when she'd begin in that wheezy voice of hers." Sephie cut into her sausage.

"There's something about the words, though."

"I suppose it's like the Catholic grace. There's tradition behind the words."

"Yes, but we don't bless the hands that made the food."

"I know. But you should."

Floyd chuckled, diving into his eggs.

As Sephie tucked into her breakfast, she squinted at Floyd.

"What?" he asked, cutting into a sausage.

"That's a different look for you."

He smiled and then tasted the sausage, adding a forkful of egg to the bite.

"Is it significant? Or just comfortable?"

The old man ran a piece of toast around the runny egg on his plate before stuffing it into his mouth.

It was unlike him to avoid an answer and that frustrated Sephie, making her testy. "Because of last night? A badge of honor? So everybody knows?"

Floyd reached a hand across the table to touch one of Sephie's. "It is significant." He smiled. "It shows I have a woman in my life. But you're supposed to do the braiding."

"Me?"

Giving her hand a tiny squeeze, he went back to his meal. "Mothers braid their sons' hair. Sisters can help if there are lots of sons. A wife braids her husband's. Sometimes men will braid each other's if they're out hunting or something."

Sephie smiled. "I do know how to braid." She, too, paid more attention to her meal. "You should have asked me to do it this morning."

He smiled again as he reached for his own cup of coffee. "You looked so peaceful sleeping. So, what do you have on the agenda to do today?"

"I think I better call a realtor. I haven't a clue who."

The old man rose from the table to pick up a piece of paper on a counter. "Well, I thought that might be one thing on your list so I pulled names from the phone book."

"What phone book? We don't have one by the phone, just a little address book because I never can remember numbers."

Sitting back down, he handed her the list. "There was one in a drawer over there." He pointed to the cabinets from where he had come. "It was pretty ragged looking. Well used. It gave me a place to start. I don't know if those realtors are still working."

Sephie squinted at the paper. She recognized familiar surnames: Singleton, Slavey, Phillips. "I think some of them are distant relatives." She chuckled. "You'd a thought the phone would be ringing off the wall, wanting to know what my plans were. The local grapevine is pretty efficient."

Floyd chuckled. "Listen to yourself. When was the last time you saw a phone on a wall?"

"1985." She said innocently.

They both laughed.

"I'll call after we eat and see who's still alive," Sephie said.

"Then what?"

Sephie took a deep breath and leaned back against her chair. "I'll start packing up Agnesia's clothes, and *you* can take them to the church."

"Me?"

"I told you. I'm not setting one foot back there." She sipped her coffee. "That reminds me. I don't think there's a Catholic church in Dark Hollow, none on this side of the state line that I remember passing by. You're under obligation, and you haven't attended since you've been helping us with the North Dakota troubles. There are no beasties or jealous wanna-be Voodoo practitioners here. You can go now."

He smiled. "That can be remedied." He sipped his coffee. "I did a search on my phone since I didn't see any listed in the phonebook. There's one in Kentucky about 20 miles away." He paused. "Will you come?"

"Of course. I have been to mass before."

"Latin?"

She chuckled. "It wasn't *that* long ago. It was actually in German. In-laws in my late husband's family in Cincinnati were Catholic. We went to a special German mass once and a few times to the regular ones. Are you afraid I'll trip when I genuflect? I do know what to do."

He smiled. "More coffee?"

She nodded.

Rising, he took her cup to the coffee pot. "Of course, that's the acculturated part of me, you know. Just like that primitive Baptist Church is yours."

"Not mine. Agnesia's. Remember my late husband was a Southern Baptist. It was a little more progressive."

"But your people? What were they?"

She shrugged. "Baptist by name with maybe a Holiness church member here and there."

"By name?" He chuckled. "Like my people. Acculturated."

"Does that make us heathens then?" she teased.

"We're like Laura and Mandy or rather they're like us. Our paths are far older."

Sephie nodded. "I still haven't gotten my soul's fill of these mountains. I think that's the only thing holding me here." That statement caused her voice to crack. She took a breath and looked up at the ceiling. "Otherwise, I'd just lock the door and tell the realtor to sell as is."

Floyd put the mug he was holding down next to Sephie's plate and stooped beside her. "You have memories here. Pictures. Keepsakes. Those have to be boxed up, and we'll take them back with us." He put his hand on her knee. "Everything else, well . . . It doesn't matter."

"I. . . ." she began.

"We'll do it together."

Chapter 8

"Well, that's the last load," Sephie said, dragging a large plastic lawn bag full of Agnesia's clothes and shoes to the front door.

"Do you want me to take this now or wait until tomorrow?"

"Now."

"Will someone be at the church at this hour?"

"Oh, yeah. They're getting ready for the Wednesday night prayer service."

Hoisting the heavy bag, he said, "Come with me. We'll take a drive into a wet county and get you a proper dinner."

She looked at him skeptically. "You researched that on your phone, too?"

He winked at her. "Come on."

Shaking her head, she gave in. "Just let me wash my face."

"I'll take this to the truck."

Sephie went to the stairs but couldn't face another climb so she diverted to the kitchen sink where she splashed water on her face and found a paper towel to dry herself off with. Remembering her purse was upstairs in her bedroom, she sighed and went to the staircase and put a foot on the first riser when she heard a loud boom upstairs.

Floyd came in at that moment. "What was that?"

Feeling the hairs on the back of her arms raise, Sephie slowly put her foot back on the floor and looked at him.

39

"A box probably fell in one of the closets," he said as he rounded her, putting his hands reassuringly on her shoulders.

"That wasn't a box falling," she said. "It sounded like someone dropped a boulder."

"I'll check."

"I'll go, too. I got to get my purse, anyway." Trying not to hold up their investigation, Sephie took the stairs a little too fast for her old bones. She was in pain by the time they searched the rooms upstairs. First, they looked in the room they'd been sharing. Nothing was amiss. They peeked into the guest bedroom. Again, nothing was out of place. When they got to Agnesia's room, they scanned basically bare space with some furniture. Her freshly-washed bedding was neatly folded and stacked on the mattress. The closet door was still ajar, exposing empty hangers and shelves. But in the middle of the room, they spied the bureau face down onto the faded, flowered linoleum.

"How'd that happen?" Floyd asked. "Did moving her clothes shift its weight or something?"

Sephie stepped in cautiously. "Sure seems strange. But old houses can be funny sometimes. Maybe the floorboards were rebounding to the lighter weight. Well, let's right this thing."

With effort, the two of them managed to pick up the top part of the bureau and swing it back upright.

"Seems mighty strange," Floyd said. "It's heavy." He then reached behind the piece of furniture and gave it a heave. He couldn't budge it without effort. "Well, that didn't come down of its own accord."

Sephie frowned, adding a shrug before she shuffled to her bedroom to find her purse.

Chapter 9

Day 3: Wednesday, Connie's Bar and Grill,
East Hollow Gap, KY, early evening

The mumble of customers and the clink of dishes could barely be heard over the belted verses of a female country singer perched on a stool in front of a microphone in the back of the restaurant. The amp had obviously been kicked to high settings. Beside her, a small bar displayed several rows of bourbon. Two beer taps were in front of the bar's counter where a bartender was pouring but wasn't using a shaker and probably wouldn't know what to do with one anyway. Most of the tables were occupied, but there wasn't a feeling of being crowded as in a club in a city where every inch of space was filled with paying clientele.

The hostess stepped from her station to greet Sephie and Floyd. "Welcome to Connie's," she said. "Two?"

"Yes, ma'am," Floyd said as he followed Sephie and the hostess to their table in a corner. The place settings were opposite each other with only one facing the music. Floyd pulled out that seat for the old woman by his side and then swiveling his chair in the corner where he could see the door and the makeshift stage.

The hostess put plastic menus in front of them and asked, "What can I get y'all to drink?"

Floyd looked at Sephie. "I know you don't like bourbon, but this may ease your aches. Do you trust me?"

She shrugged.

Turning back to the hostess. "Do you have Honey Bourbon?"

"We got Jack Daniels."

"Then bring her about four fingers of it, straight up, but it has to be ice cold."

She grinned. "We keep it in the freezer in the summer. And for you."

He smiled. "Iced tea."

The hostess raised an eyebrow. "I'll get that order in, hon. Millie will be right with you."

"Four fingers?" Sephie asked.

Floyd reached across the table and took her hand, placing it on its side, setting her little finger flush with the table. "I'm sure the bartender will measure by a small hand. Now if he used mine—" He put his hand against hers and there was room for another of Sephie's fingers and then some.

Sephie pulled her hand away. "You trying to get me drunk, old man? Even by my hand, that's too much."

"Have you taken anything for your pain today?"

She shook her head. "I was putting it off until it got too bad. I don't like eating ibuprofen like dinner mints."

Leaning back into his seat, he said, "Good. Then you can get drunk, if you want."

"How can I be sure you'll still be a gentleman?" she teased.

Before he could answer, their server, Millie, put the bourbon in front of Floyd and the iced tea in front of Sephie.

Floyd carefully switched the drinks.

Millie eyed the old woman motherly, though she had to be half her age.

Having suffered that kind of church disapproval too much lately, Sephie spoke up. "If you were in half the pain I'm in, you'd be sucking up more than this."

Millie laughed then. "Lordy, after a shift, I'm ready to down me a few, too."

Sephie took a taste of her drink expecting not to like it. It was smooth with hardly any of the oaky flavor of bourbon that she didn't like. She nodded at Floyd.

"Told you," he said but warned, "It's for sipping." Looking up at the waitress, he asked, "Do you have a special tonight?"

"Sure do, sugar. We got two. One is Mabel's liver and onions and the other is our catfish dinner."

Floyd turned an eye on Sephie, seeking her guidance.

"Is the catfish fresh?" the old woman asked.

"Yes, ma'am. It actually was fresh caught this morning. Andy, our cook, gets up at the crack of dawn and goes down by the crick. Water is clear, not muddy."

"Does he fillet it thin?" Sephie asked.

"Sure does, and he breads it in flour and cornmeal. Never tastes fishy."

"That's what I'll have," Sephie said, handing her the menu.

"You sold me," Floyd said, also handing in his menu.

"It comes with tartar sauce and a side: green beans, coleslaw, salad, or French fries."

"Are the beans cooked like Granny used to?" Sephie asked.

"'Fraid not, but they got bacon in 'em."

"Then I'll have a salad with Italian dressing."

Floyd added, "I'll have the same."

"You're an easy man to please," Millie commented.

"Well, I bow to the expert, who's from here."

Millie grinned. "Y'all want biscuits with your meal or before?"

"Before, I worked up an appetite today," the old man said.

"Be back afore long. Y'all enjoy the music." she said and left.

"'Beans like Granny used to make'?" Floyd asked.

"Cooked down all day," she explained. "Modern canned beans don't taste anything like them."

"How different are they?"

43

Taking another sip of her drink, Sephie began to feel the effects. Even though she tippled a little, it was never very much and it always hit hard. Some of the pain was easing, as well. Addressing Floyd's question, she said, "I think there may be a quart or two of beans left in the pantry that Agnesia canned last year. We should open them up and fry up some chicken tomorrow."

"I'll fry the chicken if you want, if you'll make us some biscuits."

"No, this is my meal. You never have tasted my cooking. I might send you looking for farm tomatoes though."

"I thought I saw a sign on our way here. I'll go hunting tomorrow." Floyd tasted his tea and reached for sugar in a tall clear container beside the salt and pepper shakers and a little wire rack of jelly and honey packets. Stuck between the rack and the shakers were two pieces of white paper, about a quarter of the size of one sheet. He pulled them out. One was a list of acts for Connie's Bar and Grill listed by day. Finding Wednesday, he read the performer's name and said, "That's Tennessee Lil singing."

"They have music here often?"

"Every night except Sundays when they're closed, it says here" He looked down over the list and saw a name that popped up at him. He handed the paper to Sephie. "Look at Friday night."

Sephie squinted at the typeface. Looking up, she said, "James Redman. You know him?"

"There were some Hidatsas back home named Redman."

"That's not a very original name."

He chuckled. "Neither is Whiteman. There are a couple of jazz musicians named Redman and both are Black."

"Want to go see him play?"

"It could be fun." Picking up the other piece of paper, Floyd scanned its message. "This one is about a revival. It says, 'Preacher Amos Jones, anointed with the Holy Ghost and fire,

44

will help remove hexes and get rid of haints.' A Pentecostal exorcist. I never knew there was such a thing."

"Neither did I," Sephie said, reaching for the paper.

"Think he could help with our bureau problem."

Sephie harrumphed. "It's not a hex or a haint." Returning to the paper, she noticed something else and handed the paper back to Floyd.

"Look down at the bottom."

Floyd raised an eyebrow as he read: With special music by James Redman. "He's a diverse musician, I guess."

"When's the revival start?"

"Actually, it's been running for two weeks. Its last night is tomorrow."

"Well now, seems we found our evening entertainment for the next couple of nights," Sephie announced.

Chapter 10

Day 3: Wednesday, Sephie's home,
Dark Hollow TN, late evening

Tucked comfortably in Sephie's black, wrought iron bed, she and Floyd had just turned off the light and were cuddled against each other.

"Feel better, old woman?" Floyd asked.

"You were right about the bourbon. My bones don't ache so much, but I don't want to live with liquor in the house."

"Worried about me going off the wagon?"

"No, you've settled that in your spirit. You don't behave like. . . ." She couldn't say the word.

"An alcoholic?" He pulled her closer. "I may have looked like one, but I really was chasing something. Anything. I just don't need it now. I don't need the wandering. The travel or the wandering eye."

"You can't place your sobriety on someone else."

He shifted so he could caress her face in the dim moonlight coming from the window. "I'm not," he said, before kissing her. "But you are my lodestone and my anchor. Whatever happens, I'll always come back to you. Always."

"You can't promise that at our age."

"Always," he said again and kissed her one last time, finally settling back into the bed and pulling her close.

Sephie rested her head on his shoulder with her arm across his chest. She was puzzled by his statement but also comforted, willing to leave the mysteries of life to those wiser than she was. As Sephie finally slipped into sleep, a loud BAM resounded in the room.

Startled, Floyd shifted to sit up. "Was that the bureau?"

"Leave it till morning," Sephie said.

As Floyd settled back down beside her, he wondered aloud, "Still think we don't have a haint?"

Sephie sighed. "I'm going to call a junk store and have them come and pick up all of Agnesia's furniture."

"Wise."

Chapter 11

Rinsing off the dirty dishes from Sephie's fried chicken dinner, Floyd announced, "I thought all you southern gals deep fried your chicken."

"I don't want to put another husband in the ground from a heart attack," Sephie said, taking the plates and putting them in the dishwasher. "I quit deep frying after my husband had his first heart attack. It helped, but he already had 55 years of eating like that, even way before I met him." She straightened and said, "I'd like to keep your face around a while longer."

He smiled and pulled her close before handing her their silverware. "I'm glad you have a dishwasher."

"For years, I did it all by hand. Then before Agnesia moved in, I took some of Earl's insurance money and had it installed. I thought I'd give myself one luxury. But Agnesia commandeered the kitchen, and I really never got to use it." She bent down to tap Floyd's knees in front of the sink cabinet doors. When he moved, she pulled out the liquid detergent and filled the reservoir in the door of the dishwasher. Before closing it, Sephie looked around to see if they had forgotten anything. This load had taken three days to fill since they had had reheated meals on paper plates from the church ladies.

Replacing the detergent under the sink, she said, "I think that's it." She slid the lock on the dishwasher and turned it on. There was click, then the sound of water running. Sephie reached to wash her hands at the sink, as Floyd dried his.

The dishwasher emitted a growl of noise that sounded like voices from the gates of Hell.

Sephie jumped back against Floyd, stepping on the toe of his boot. "It's speaking in tongues!"

Floyd backed away, pulling her with him. "It's probably some air in the water pipes to the dishwasher. That can happen in old houses."

"Maybe we should salt it or smudge it."

"We'd need to smudge the whole house. We don't have time before the revival service. But we should smudge before we leave to go back to ND."

Sephie rushed to the table, grabbed the salt shaker, and unscrewed the lid. She poured some into her hand and tossed it at the machine. The dishwasher continued to growl and mumble as the sound of water continued. Suddenly, what came from the machine was the normal purring of the spray of the machine.

Both Sephie and Floyd took a deep breath and stared at each other.

"Maybe church is the best place for us tonight," Sephie said.

Chapter 12

Day 4: Thursday, revival tent,
outside of East Hollow Gap, KY, early evening

From their wooden folding seats in the front row on the left side of the white revival tent, Sephie and Floyd had a good view of Preacher Amos Jones. He was a portly man in his 50s, wearing a white suit with suspenders showing across the front of his white, open-collared shirt. There was no tie and no tie clip or any other jewelry, not even a wedding ring. He paused often in the cadence of his preaching to wipe his bald head with a generous, white handkerchief.

The music that began the service was led by a song leader and a handful of people, singing ageless gospel hymns that Sephie remembered from her childhood. They were much livelier ones than those sung at Agnesia's church. Tonight, these were songs that everybody knew. Beginning with "Blessed Assurance," the songs became more upbeat, getting everybody up on their feet and clapping to the rhythms, often in double claps or counter rhythms. Each song ran into the next as they sang through a repertory of "Wings of a Dove," "I'll Fly Away," "I Saw the Light," "Everybody's Gonna Have a Wonderful Time Up There," and "Down by the Riverside."

Unlike the music at the Church in the Valley, these songs were accompanied by a simple pit band consisting of a drummer with a full kit, a bass player, a rhythm guitar player, and an electric lead guitar player. All of the stringed instruments were plugged in to amplifiers so that the music echoed off the surrounding hills and could be heard from their location on the edge of town into the country streets of East Hollow Gap, probably competing with the music at Connie's Bar & Grill.

The lead guitar player was obviously native. He was dressed in a pale blue shirt, black jeans, and black leather boots. On his head was a black Stetson hat like the one Floyd wore, but this one had a thin, beaded band with two beaded tassels. He also wore two dangling beaded earrings, something that she was sure Preacher Amos didn't approve of.

Sephie glanced up at Floyd to see how he took it all in. The old man eagerly joined in on the clapping and singing the songs he knew, offering a rich tenor that often was laced with harmonies. Sephie managed her own alto, switching from the melody to a harmony of her own. In the crowd that gathered, it was easy to listen to other voices and try to slip in something that might fit.

The preaching was what Sephie had expected, equally lively, and with that time-honed evangelical vocal cadence. It was often interspersed with speaking in tongues, a holy language Sephie had heard many times at Holiness Churches. Preacher Amos spoke of sin and redemption, told stories about how he was a drunkard before he found the Lord, and urged people to look within. But instead of calling people to the mourner's bench to repent, he paused, caught his breath, wiped his face and his head again, and then looked off to his left.

"Tonight. Tonight, brothers and sisters, I want to show you the power of faith. We have with us tonight Brother Eustice Phillips and his daughter Flossie. Brother Eustace is still doin' God's work even though his sight's failing."

A tall thin man in his 60s shuffled up the steps at the side of the low stage. He was dressed in khaki pants and a white shirt, open-collared like the preacher's, with his sleeves rolled up to his bony elbows. Clutching one of those elbows was a woman in her forties, dressed in a long, dark blue skirt and a long-sleeved white blouse. Her hair was also long, reaching down her back to below her behind. She wore no makeup or jewelry, just very small, wire-rimmed glasses.

Preacher Amos met Eustace and guided him to the center of the stage, where the lighting from the scaffolding was the most intense. The preacher turned him to face the congregation and everyone gasped. The right side of the older man's face drooped, the lower lip pushed out and down as if he'd had a stroke. His eye, though, was squished shut. Scars from snakebites decorated his cheek, jaw, neck, and along his arm and hand, which hung limply.

Preacher Amos pushed a portable microphone into Brother Eustace's left hand. "Brothers and sisters," he slurred, making what he said nearly impossible to understand. "We come here tonight to give witness to faith. Mark 16:17 says—"

"And these signs shall follow them that believe," Preacher Amos interrupted. "In my name shall they cast out devils, they shall speak with new tongues, they shall take up serpents, and if they drink any deadly thing, it shall not hurt them; they shall lay hands on the sick, and they shall recover."

Flossie left the stage to bring a wire case to her father's feet. The reddish brown and gray contents writhed.

With Preacher Amos' help, Brother Eustace shakily reached down to raise the lid as the pit band started playing. The lead guitar player, his head down, didn't join in, but draped his right arm over his strings and surreptitiously made the sign of the cross, kissing the knuckle of his forefinger with his left hand.

Sephie looked at Floyd, who was doing the same thing. She added a prayer of safety of her own.

Not only did Brother Eustace bring out a copperhead in his left hand and put it into his right but, he also grabbed a rattler in his left. His grip wasn't as secure on the copperhead since he could barely lift the injured limb just enough to keep it away from his thigh.

Sephie winced as Floyd gripped her wrist. He leaned over to whisper, "Move if I nudge you." She nodded. There was an open space of only about ten feet from the stage and their folding chairs.

Brother Eustace raised the rattlesnake high above his head as he shuffled to the music. He could only wave the copperhead back and forth while Flossie clapped, praising God and slipping into tongues with her arms open wide as if to receive the blessings of belief.

The congregation grew louder as the excitement in the tent escalated. The pit band kept up a consistent but hypnotic beat, while worshipers stood, sometimes spilling out into the aisles to dance in ecstasy while shouting praises as their arms and torsos jerked with the holy anointing.

Sephie stiffened in her seat, watching the serpents try to coil in reaction to the noise. Brother Eustace had them by the middle of their bodies, not just past the head as she'd seen on nature shows. There was room for them to twist enough to bite one of his hands as he continued to shuffle and shout some message that was totally unintelligible. It wasn't the heavenly language she had heard during this service and at other Pentecostal churches. It was purely the man's neurological inability to speak clearly.

The old woman felt Floyd's body also tense beside her as he removed his hand from her wrist and swung his arm around her shoulders. They were vulnerable if Brother Eustace's hold on either snake loosened and the vipers slithered across the dirt floor toward them. Sephie looked down at Floyd's leather boots, which had much better protection than her black, suede slippers. She nervously looked up at his face, which was alert but hard as if carved in stone, and felt not only her mortality but his as well. Closing her eyes, she grabbed the old man's free hand and prayed to Spirit and all of the beings of the land where the tent had been erected, asking for their protection not only for Floyd and herself but also for everyone there. Sephie even sent apologies to the snakes. She chanted, "Protect us, protect us, protect us."

Feeling Floyd's breath in her ear, she stopped chanting as she heard him add a chant of his own in his own language.

There were loud cries of "Hallelujah!" and "Praise God!" from the congregation before the band stopped playing. Looking up, they saw the snakes safely in their cage and Preacher Amos once again mopping his bald head with his handkerchief.

"Hallelujah!" the preacher said, "We have all witnessed the power of faith in the Lord. Thank you, Brother Eustace, for bringing this miracle and being a vessel for it."

The snake handler did a final shuffle dance with his left arm raised as he shouted something. He then let Flossie lead him down the side steps of the stage to empty folding chairs nearby.

Relieved, Sephie leaned against Floyd, who pulled her close. The altar call and final hymn were a blur.

Finally, Preacher Amos said, "This is our last night here in East Hollow Gap. We'll be up in Somerset starting tomorrow night. So, tell your friends and relatives to come out and witness the power of the Lord. See miracles and get saved." He grinned as he crossed the stage to the band. "We want to especially thank a gentleman, who helped us with our revival band for the past week. We lost one of our guitar players at our last town so we were really glad to find a replacement here." Leaning down toward the lead guitarist, Preacher Amos asked, "Give us a testimony about your experience here."

When the microphone was shoved in his face, the musician squinted at the preacher and then out at the congregation. He leaned into the microphone and spoke in a native language.

Floyd put his head down and covered his mouth, making Sephie furrow her forehead at him.

Then the musician looked up at the preacher and said, "Swift journey."

The preacher grinned. "Let's all give him a big round of applause."

Chapter 13

The congregation cleared the tent after Preacher Amos' final "And may God bless you!" Floyd and Sephie left their chairs to climb the three steps on the left side of the stage to approach the musicians, who were packing up their instruments and unplugging microphones and amplifiers. The lead guitarist looked up as he snapped the locks on his rectangular, black hard-shell guitar case. Standing, he waited with his arms crossed.

Floyd surveyed how far away the other musicians were before he chuckled and said, "I agree with what you said."

The musician raised an eyebrow but didn't say a word.

"Hidatsa?" the old man asked.

The young man's mouth fell open, then shut it as he studied Floyd. "You, too?"

Floyd nodded. "Mandan mixed."

The musician extended his hand, "James Redman."

"Floyd Whiteman."

James laughed. "We both had very uninventive ancestors, didn't we?"

"What brings you so far from home?"

"I could ask you the same thing," James said.

Floyd put his arm around Sephie. "A good woman. This is Sephie. I met her back home."

James offered his hand to the old woman and gently shook her fingers, not her whole hand, a sign of respect. "Ma'am," he said. Turning back to Floyd, he answered his question. "I've been touring, trying to make enough to get back home. I took this gig for the extra money. It's hard for a solo blues player."

Floyd nodded. "I saw that you were playing tomorrow at Connie's."

"I'm just getting tips there. It's a tiny place. This gig at least had a guarantee for two weeks."

"Can we buy you dinner or something? I can tell you news about home."

James smiled, but hesitated, finally nodding. "Thank you."

"Connie's okay?"

"Sure. Just let me get my pay. I'll get a ride there."

"We can wait."

James shook his head.

Floyd nodded, then offered his hand again.

Chapter 14

Day 4: Thursday, Connie's Bar & Grill,
East Hollow Gap, KY, late evening

The ice cream melted quickly on the warm piece of apple pie as Floyd sawed off a forkful. Beside him, Sephie nibbled at her slice of rhubarb pie. "Any good?" he asked her.

"A tad too sweet," she remarked. "You want some tang or it's not rhubarb." She took a sip of her decaf and commented. "The boy seems lost. He's a long way from home."

Floyd nodded. "I wonder. . . ."

Sephie touched his hand. "We should. He's family or close to it."

Squeezing her hand, he smiled. "You're a good woman."

"We could use some help. I don't want you twisting something that you can't get fixed here." Returning to her pie, she added, "I don't think I can remember how to drive a stick shift. I want to see that place of yours sometime before Spring."

Floyd chuckled, cutting off another forkful of pie.

"Sorry," a voice said, causing the old man to look up.

James pulled out a chair in front of him and sat.

"Did you get your money?"

He nodded, picking up the menu in front of him that had a sheet paperclipped to the front. James frowned over it.

"How long you been in this town, James?"

"Almost a month now. I had some trouble with my truck."

Sipping his own coffee, Floyd asked, "Is it running now?"

Bypassing the question, the young man put the menu down and waved down Millie, who sauntered over and took his order for an open-faced roast beef sandwich and iced tea.

When she had gone, Floyd pressed, "Your truck still in the garage?"

James ran his finger over the scared wooden table as the silence lengthened.

"Son," Sephie began gently, "how long since you've seen your family?"

Raising his eyes to look at hers, he admitted, "Five years, ma'am. I had stars in my eyes. I left with a blues band that said it had a bunch of gigs all lined up. They did for a while: Fargo, Minneapolis, Racine, outside of Chicago, Indianapolis, Bloomington, Cincinnati, Newport, Kentucky. Then the lead singer got busted for cocaine, and we tried to keep touring, playing happy hours. People want to hear lyrics not just music. We could only get little gigs in small towns and that's hard sometimes when people in the South just want to hear country. So, when the other guys called it quits, I tried to make a go of it on my own. I was pretty versatile and could play mostly anything, but I'm not a singer. I was working my way North after playing a tourist bar in Gatlinburg when my engine blew a gasket here."

Millie brought James his meal, smothered in brown gravy. "You want that on your tab, hon?"

"We got it," Floyd said.

She nodded and sashayed off to sweet talk other customers.

"Where have you been staying?" Sephie asked.

"I got a room over the bar. They take rent and food out so that's why I'm only getting tips. I play at one of the churches, too, and they pay me out of the collection plate." James looked down at his hot meal but seemed to have to lost his taste for it.

"Did you sign a contract to play here?" Floyd asked.

James shook his head. "Not in a place like this."

Floyd drank from his mug. When he put it down, he looked over at Sephie, who dipped her head just once. "You need to get back home," Floyd stated.

"I know," James said. Taking in a deep breath, he picked up his knife and fork and cut into the roast beef. He chewed the meat as if he were gnawing on the stringiness of the last five bitter years.

Floyd wiped his mouth with his napkin. "Tell you what, James. I'll come up tomorrow before noon, and we'll take a look at your truck."

"Won't do any good," James admitted. "They won't start work until I have the cash in hand. And I don't have near enough yet."

"You got any sentiment attached to that vehicle? Like did your uncle give it to you?"

The young man laughed. "I picked up that old junker in Louisville on my way to Gatlinburg. I'm surprised it's stayed in one piece. But it's all I got."

Sephie smiled. "James, you can go back home with us in about a month, if you want."

Surprised, Floyd turned to the old woman. "Will that be enough time?"

"If we had help, it could be sooner." She turned to James. "We could sure use some help."

James narrowed his eyes. "Doing what?"

"We're packing up, getting a house ready to sell," Floyd said. "I'm strong yet, but I could use a couple of extra hands. Let's go look at your truck tomorrow and see where we are."

Sephie reached a hand to one of James'. "We've got a spare room, too."

James sat back against his chair. "I-I can't. . . ."

"We probably have a mutual cousin somewhere," Floyd said. "You're family."

Finally, James grinned. "Do you know Old Man Wilkie?"

"The carver, whose wife makes moccasins with fancy beadwork for the Powwows? Yep. He's related to my late wife. Did you hear about his mean old dog that he'd tried to train for years but finally died?"

The young man stared seriously at Floyd. "He made leather out of its hide for his wife."

"He told me it was the most use that worthless animal had in its whole life."

James nodded. "It was. Meanest dog I ever saw."

"How're you kin?"

James finally smiled. "He's my great uncle." James dug heartily into his roast beef sandwich, seeming to savor every mouthful.

Chapter 15

Day 5: Friday, Sephie's home,
Dark Hollow, TN, morning

"I don't want you climbing those stairs while I'm gone," Floyd said, pouring coffee into a thermos. "Start sorting down here somewhere and making piles."

"I'm not feeble," Sephie argued, taking their breakfast plates to the sink.

"I'm not saying you are, but you don't need to strain yourself." He screwed on the lid of the thermos and then the mug top. "I'll try to find some boxes and packing tape."

"I gotta call the realtor and see if she knows a good used furniture store that can pick up the big pieces."

"We definitely need to remove your sister's furniture. I'm tired of trying to tip that bureau up on its end every morning."

Sephie chuckled. "If that really is Agnesia showing her disapproval, I just wonder exactly how much we can take back with us. Her energy must've seeped through everything."

Eyeing the dishwasher, Floyd asked, "You think that was her in there?"

The old woman shrugged. "Don't know. She never thought much of speaking in tongues."

Scanning the kitchen, Floyd said, "We won't need dishes or pots and pans, though I would like those big iron skillets. Is there something special you wanted?"

"I'd like Grandma's bowl that she made biscuits in."

"The flowered one you've been using?"

She nodded.

"We'll smudge it and pack it in salt. We may have to do

the same with the skillets." He smiled at her. "We can do that with any dishes you want."

Sephie sighed and shook her head. "Maybe a piece or two like a gravy boat. It's nothing fancy." Looking around the room, she decided, "I'll work in here today. This really is the room where Agnesia spent most of her time and where things would be most imprinted. And it's probably the only room in the house with the most stuff because my sister and I combined all of our kitchen things."

Floyd put his arms around Sephie. "Are you going to be all right doing this alone?"

She nodded. "It's only stuff."

Bending down, he kissed her. "I'll be back by lunch time. I'll bring some cold cuts and cheese so lunch will be easy. And I'll see where I can find you some more farm tomatoes."

"Stay safe, old man."

He grinned, picked up his thermos, and headed for the door.

Sephie put her hands on her hips, as she slowly developed a strategy for her big chore. She'd pull out the skillets and Grandma's bowl and then basic things to continue to cook meals with. Everything else would be stacked on the table and counters, ready for packing.

As she stooped to the warming drawer under the stove to pull out the skillets, a loud BAM! stopped her in her tracks. She straightened, trying to figure out where the sound had come from. It hadn't been from upstairs. It sounded close by. Slowly, she turned in a circle to look at every angle of the kitchen. Nothing was out of place.

The old woman first went to the big walk-in pantry where Agnesia kept the fruits of her canning. Sephie opened the door and pulled the chain on the naked bulb in the socket on the ceiling. As light filled the room, she looked on the floor. It was clear. There was really only one shelf of food left; the rest of the space was filled with empty Mason jars, a big, water-bath canner, and a monstrous pressure canner. By this time each year, those shelves would begin to be filled with green beans, tomatoes, pickled beets, and even peaches. Sephie realized just how much Agnesia's health had obviously affected her production. Sighing, Sephie looked for exploded jars but found none. That used to happen when she was a child due to some bacteria in the jars because they hadn't been sterilized properly or weren't processed enough. Nothing was out of place.

Sephie moved to the other side of the room and opened the laundry room door. On the floor was a jug of liquid detergent, its contents oozing from the lid. The wire shelf above the washer and dryer combo held another jug of detergent, a jug of bleach, and two boxes of dryer sheets. A two-inch metal lip running the length of the shelf secured the laundry supplies so they wouldn't fall. Yet, somehow the jug had been elevated over the lip and onto the floor.

Normally, the old woman would have immediately stepped inside, picked up jug, and found a mop or cloth to wipe up the spill. A cold shiver running down Sephie's spine, however, caused her to back away and close the door. She'd wait until Floyd returned, and they'd both tackle the mess.

Chapter 16

Day 5: Friday, Sephie's home,
Dark Hollow, TN, near noon

Wiping her face with a paper towel, Sephie surveyed her work. Dishes covered nearly every surface in the kitchen with no seeming reason for what was in each stack or why they were grouped on specific surfaces. The old woman had carefully thought things out though. Only the small counters on each side of the stove held items that would be packed for transport back to North Dakota. Everything else was destined to go to either the First Baptist Church Thrift Store or an antique store in La Follette. She was ready for a rest but noticed that it was almost twelve o'clock. She put fresh water in the coffee maker and measured out dark roast into a filter. She'd just punched the ON switch when she heard a knock at the front door.

Her eyes beseeching heaven that it wasn't more church ladies, Sephie shuffled out to the living room to pull the solid core door open. On the welcome mat stood a tall, gangly man in his fifties, his hair looking freshly buzz cut, and bearing a smile with a gap between his two front teeth. He was dressed in khaki pants and a white shirt.

Beside him was a woman near his age, dressed in a navy polyester summer dress bedecked with lighter blue flowers. Her short, blonde hair was lacquered into a helmet that accentuated her high cheekbones, the dark blue eye shadow she wore, and her bright red lipstick. Over one arm hung a black leather handbag while the hand grasped a cloth tote.

"T. Berry, Easter," Sephie greeted them. "I thought you were still traveling."

"We just got back, Cousin Sephie," Easter said, leaning to give the older woman a brief almost unfelt kiss on the cheek. "Otherwise, we'd have been to the funeral."

"You can't tell the captain of a cruise ship to speed up," T. Berry said.

"Well, come on in. I just put on some coffee."

They entered, and T. Berry settled on the cream and gold striped sofa.

"I brought you a blackberry cobbler," Easter said, following Sephie into the kitchen. "And some ice cream. I'd never had it before, but one of the grandkids' friend's mom serves it like that so I tried it." She pulled out a quart of Old-Fashioned Vanilla from her tote. "And, you know, I really liked it." She jerked open the freezer door of the fridge and shoved the carton into the compartment that held bagged meat and chicken neatly stacked in a corner. Removing a plastic container from the tote, she put that inside the refrigerator.

Sephie started to pull out mugs from the dishes she had reserved on the counter by the coffeemaker but then realized she'd need another when Floyd came back. Diverting to the kitchen table, she picked up three matching cups and saucers. They weren't fancy, but they were good enough for company.

Taking them to the coffeemaker, she saw Easter hurry back to the kitchen doorway. The younger woman stretched her neck to look toward the living room. Rushing back into the kitchen, she went to the pantry door, opened it, and then pulled something else out of the tote to place on a shelf. She shut the door and joined Sephie at the coffeemaker. "Cousin Lige brought over a quart of shine for you," she said, pulling out a drawer to find silverware.

"I'm not making tinctures now. Besides, my whole supply is up at Mandy's store."

Putting sugar and non-dairy creamer into one cup, Easter explained, "This is something special he made for you. It's for sipping. It's butterscotch shine."

"Flavored moonshine?" Sephie was stunned.

"Well, the big liquor stores in Knoxville have all kinds of flavored bourbons and even legal moonshine. So, Lige wanted to try and make some. He gave me a taste." She looked around guiltily and then began adding creamer to another cup. "Lordy, keep that away from me. It's so good, but it'll take you down a badger hole. Mercy!" Easter picked up the two cups she had doctored and headed back to the living room.

Sephie followed with her lone cup of black coffee before sitting down in a cream-colored wing chair on the left side of the sofa. When she put her cup and saucer on the coffee table with both hands, Easter grabbed her left hand.

"Are you still pining for your husband?"

"No, I—"

Floyd opened the front door with James Redman following.

Sephie started to rise, but Floyd waved her down with his left hand before placing it on her shoulder. "Floyd, these are my second cousins, T. Berry Jeffers and his wife Easter."

The old man removed his hand from Sephie's shoulder, moved a plastic grocery bag to it, and extended his right hand to T. Berry, who had risen. "I'm Sephie's—."

"Of course, ya are," the younger man gave him a warm, gap-toothed grin as he shook hands. "Welcome to the family." Noticing the much younger man with Floyd, he asked, "He your son?"

Floyd smiled slowly. "My . . . cousin . . . James.

Suddenly, T. Berry's phone clanged. It wasn't a beep, a buzz, or even a song ringtone. It was a loud, old-fashioned fire department bell. Stepping away, T. Berry took the call.

Noticing the grocery bags in Floyd and James' free hands, Sephie got to her feet. "Let me put that away." Before she could though, T. Berry swaggered back to everyone, his eyes glistening with excitement.

"They's been a shootin' over in Whitetree." He hitched up his pants. "Wanna go over yonder?"

Floyd opened his mouth to respond, but T. Berry added. "I'll give you a tour of the county. You'll see what you're marryin' into."

"We can't be away too long," Floyd finally said. "I need to get some food into the boy before we tackle a project."

"The county ain't that big. We'll be back in an hour. . . . Unless the crime scene gets interestin'."

Sephie took the bags from James and then Floyd, who bent down to kiss her cheek. "Any advice?" he whispered.

"Don't divorce me yet," she said, heading for the kitchen.

"Let me help you with that," Easter said, following. "T. Berry likes to keep his fingers in police business," she explained as Sephie placed the plastic bags on the counter by the coffeemaker and removed tomatoes from one. "He really misses being chief of police in West Virginia. But he lost the last election." Easter pulled out sesame seeded buns from the other bag. "Frankly, I'm glad. Though he never had to go on patrol, I still worried about him getting shot." She removed a plastic bag of deli ham and another of Colby cheese. "'Course, T. Berry's trucking company has him making command decisions, and he likes that." She turned to the table. "We're gonna have to move all that if we're gonna feed the men in here. I don't know how y'all managed holidays without a separate dining room."

Sephie sighed. She really didn't have anywhere to put those dishes except back into the cabinets.

A noise drew the older woman's attention. His line of sight blocked by a stack of boxes in his arms, James had bumped into the doorway. Sephie shuffled over to remove two of them and place them on the floor out of the way.

"We got more in the truck, but they can stay there until we get back. Floyd just thought you might want a start. There's packing tape and a marker in one of these."

"Thanks, James. This was a solution to a puzzle."

He nodded, but hesitated, puzzled himself. "Um, Floyd told me to tell you: Never."

Sephie chuckled. "Hurry back. We'll fix you a good meal."

When James had left, Sephie searched the boxes for the packing tape and the marker. She also found one box full of newspapers. The old woman picked one up and found it was last week's edition. "You can clear that table by packing those dishes for me," Sephie said. "I'll see what I can pull together."

"It'll have to be more than sandwiches. T. Berry likes a hot meal. You got any canned beans? Those tomatoes and that light bread made me think of breaded tomatoes."

"Don't touch my tomatoes. I'll see if there are any canned ones left in the pantry," Sephie said, turning to the walk-in storage closet.

"Y'all might as well taste Cousin Lige's brew while you're in there," Easter called after her as she pulled out a chair and put a box on it.

In the pantry, Sephie found a quart of tomatoes. Breaded tomatoes were tasty. She hadn't had them in a long while. Agnesia had only used her canned ones for plain stewed tomatoes, which she always ruined by putting sugar in them when she served them. There was also one last quart of beans tucked into the back of the shelf. She also found a pint of chow chow and one of pickled beets. Arms full, Sephie struggled out of the pantry and barely made it to the counter where groceries had been placed. She noticed that Easter had dived into her task with efficiency and nary a grumble.

While the old woman washed her hands at the sink, she asked, "How're your grandkids?"

Wrapping another plate in newspaper, Easter said with pride, "Daryl got a real good job down in Nashville with a marketing company after he graduated. And Carla is doing a summer art program at Vanderbilt."

"They sound like they finally found themselves," Sephie said, drying her hands.

"Well, it was a little rocky there for a while after their folks died," Easter said. "Who'd a thought cancer would take one and a heart attack the other so quickly after. At least, T. Berry got his police buddies to reduce that auto theft charge to joyriding so it didn't reflect on the background checks for Daryl's job applications."

"That's good," the old woman said, picking up one of the iron skillets she had set aside and putting it on the stove. She then found a pot for the beans.

"And Carla got clean last year. She found art was a better outlet than tripping. Though those paintin's of hers sure look like a weird trip."

"Oh really?" Sephie remarked almost shaking her head at her cousin's report. She picked up the quart jar of beans and attacked the lid.

"Say, is Floyd, you know. . . ."

Sephie twisted her head to look at her, wondering if she was going to make some remark about him being native.

"You know. . . . A widower?"

Chuckling, Sephie applied herself to the canning lid but couldn't budge it. "Yes," she said, "a few years ago." Offering the jar to her cousin, she said, "Can you?"

"Well, a man that handsome couldn't have been single all his life," Easter said, taking the jar. She turned it upside down and slammed the lid on the counter, righted it, and then applied some muscle to the jar ring, which easily twisted free. "Let me do the other'uns, too."

"Thanks," Sephie said. Using the hook on a can opener, she quickly flipped the canning lid off the jar of beans and dumped the contents into the pot.

Easter applied the same tactics to all of the jars Sephie had brought out, and their jar rings easily twisted off. "Where did y'all meet him? Up North?"

Sephie nodded, lighting the burner under the beans and turning it on low. "He's a good friend of Mandy and Laura's."

"How's their store doing?"

"Seems to be doing all right," Sephie said, lighting the burner under the iron skillet before she added the canned tomatoes. "They know a lot of nice people up there."

"Didn't you drive up with some college kid?"

Adding black pepper to the tomatoes, Sephie said, "Yeah. B.D. Nice boy. He's staying up there, got a job singing at a restaurant and for some churches. He's thinking about doing his Master's up there. They got different songs than what he found here and back in his hometown."

"When we heard that you were thinking of driving up there by yourself, we just couldn't imagine it."

"I'm capable," Sephie insisted, pulling out two buns from the bag of eight.

"Yes, but it's a long way for a woman alone. I wouldn't do it."

Turning to Easter, she asked, "When was the last time you drove any distance by yourself?"

Easter stopped wrapping a plate with newspaper and seemed to blink. "I — well, I don't remember. I mean I drive all over Dark Hollow and I did drive to La Follette once or twice before T. Berry and I got married."

"That's what? Forty miles?" Sephie asked.

"Well, how far did you ever drive by yourself?"

Sephie stirred the tomatoes with a wooden spoon and then started tearing the bread into small pieces and adding them to the pan. "Well, I drove up to Louisville a couple of times after Earl passed so I could see Debra and Joe. That was before they moved to Atlanta. I was gonna drive there a couple of years ago, but Debra got wind of it. She squawked like the over-protective daughter she can be sometimes. I met her and Joe in Gatlinburg." She stirred the bread into the tomatoes. "I really think Debra just wanted to have a vacation and go to all those tourist shops."

Easter laughed. "I don't blame her. I love Gatlinburg!" Placing the final plate in the box, she asked, "Do y'all want this sealed up?"

"Just label it, *Plates*, and just crisscross the lid. You know what I mean. Those are going to the First Baptist Church Thrift store."

"The thrift store? I wouldn't of packed them so good. I thought y'all were taking them back with you."

Shaking her wooden spoon at her, she scolded, "Those plates can do a family some good. They don't need to get all chipped because it's for charity. Neither Agnesia or I had very much that was worth anything. Except maybe Grandma's biscuit bowel because it's so old, not because it's valuable in itself."

Easter shook her head and started tucking the box lids into a weave pattern that would seal the box but allow it to be easily opened.

Sephie returned to the stove and stuck the spoon into the pot of green beans to give them a stir. She was debating on adding a tiny pinch of sugar to the beans when a shriek made her jump.

Swinging on Easter, thinking she saw a spider in one of the boxes, Sephie was ready to calm her down. The younger woman was backing away from the table, pointing to something on the floor on the other side. Stepping to her left, Sephie saw movement. A gray, airy wad about the size of a tennis ball was twitching back and forth as if indecisive where to go — or hunting. It moved toward Easter, twitched. The young woman pulled herself up on a chair, emitting another shriek. The thing then headed toward Sephie, where it darted toward her, causing the old woman to sidle farther to the left. The ball twitched again and moved toward Sephie, who moved to her right. Quickly moving farther right and then changing direction to the left, she stepped forward toward the pantry door. The thing changed direction again and kept the old woman in focus. Sephie took mincing steps around the thing until she had her back toward the pantry where she'd left the door open. The thing darted toward her and Sephie stepped aside when it was just inches away, letting the object speed past her. She quickly slammed the door shut, securing it with her backside.

Panting in panic, Easter climbed down from the chair and said, "I never in all my life thought I'd ever see one."

"What?" Sephie asked, unsure what she had actually seen. It looked like a gray dust bunny but a big one.

"A witch ball!"

"That's just a story."

"You call what just ran through this kitchen a story? That was a witch ball. They're made of the hair from the witch that sent it to you. Who'd want to hex you?"

Sephie tried to reason with her. "No one's wanting to hex me." Feeling that the thing was secure behind the pantry door, she made her way to a cabinet to one side of the stove where she kept seasonings. The old woman pulled out a box of salt. "We'll just keep whatever is in there inside." She waved Easter away and laid down a line of salt right under the edge of the door. "That should hold it for a long while."

Marching back to the stove, she asked, "Who told you it was made from a witch's hair?"

"Granny Chitwood."

"That old woman was full of tales," Sephie said, putting the salt away and closing the cabinet door. "She said it was hexing?"

"Sure did. And you can't let it touch you or you'll get red burn marks where it did. She called it a witch bullet."

Sephie squinted, as if that would help her remember that old tale. "I heard once it was made of hair, all right, but not the witch's. It could be made from anybody's hair. That's why we were always told to be careful with getting a haircut or cleaning our combs and brushes. We had to dispose of it."

"I was told that, too," Easter said. "We had to throw it in the fire."

"Is that how you get rid of that thing?"

"Yep. You gotta burn it."

"If we can catch it again," Sephie said.

Easter looked at the old woman, and Sephie looked back. "Let's let the men folk deal with it," Easter said.

Realizing Floyd might be the better person to deal with something like this anyway, Sephie deferred to his ignorance or his possible knowledge of this particular phenomenon. Either would probably protect him. "I think you're right, Easter. I'll let Floyd handle it."

Chapter 17

"I was surprised you wanted to come with me when I dropped James off at Connie's to practice for his show after all that company you had. I thought you'd want some peace and quiet."

Sephie nestled a little closer to Floyd on the truck's bench seat. "I needed some space. And the energy you and James have. It's quieter. But I may just pass on going to see James play tonight."

Putting his arm around her, he let silence surround them as Sephie put her head on his shoulder.

"How'd James handle T. Berry's shooting?"

Letting out a low rumbling chuckle, he said, "That boy has led a sheltered life."

Sephie raised her head to look at him. "What do you mean?"

"He was raised on the rez, sure. But it's quiet out there mostly. We have an incident maybe once in a decade or so. It's not like a big city or out here as I far as I can tell. And usually the same kind of thing: a domestic issue. And everybody has a rifle for hunting."

"And?" Sephie prompted.

Again, Floyd chuckled. "James was up front in that big boat of a car your cousin drives."

"Yeah, he likes those old Oldsmobiles and town cars."

"Well, James was trying to put on his seatbelt and ended up grabbing the butt of a loaded pistol your cousin had stuffed down between the seats. The way he jumped I thought one of those copperheads from last night had gotten loose." He chuckled. "We just don't treat guns so casual."

"No one should," Sephie muttered, settling back against Floyd.

"That's not all. T. Berry kept looking back at me in the back seat while he was driving through these mountain roads. James was hanging on as if his life depended on it. And maybe it did. There were drop offs on each side of some of those ridge roads we were on."

"At least you both got back in one piece."

"I almost choked when T. Berry pulled up to the officer trying to keep people out of the way. He rolled down his window and the first thing he said was, 'Anybody get killed?'" Finding the turn off down to Sephie's house, Floyd added, "It was a domestic dispute. A guy was drunk, and his wife tried to chase him off with a shotgun so the neighbors called the sheriff."

"Well, at least no one got hurt, and James broadened his education," Sephie said, then added cryptically, "I wish a shotgun was an easy remedy to chase off what we got."

As the truck coasted to a stop in front of her house. "Something else happen?"

Sephie eased away from Floyd and undid her seatbelt. "I need your help with these," she said, opening the door and sliding down onto the ground.

Quickly getting out and rounding on Sephie at the front of the truck, Floyd gently took her elbow to get her to stop. "These? More than one?"

She nodded. "Two. I don't know that this is all Agnesia." Squinting up at him, she added, "The bureau, yes, that's Agnesia. I think the reason she didn't come around when we got here is that she was busy enjoying the mourning from the church biddies."

"And we hadn't. . . ." Floyd left the description of their intimacy unsaid.

Sephie waggled her head toward one shoulder then the next. "She definitely didn't approve."

"So, what do we have now?"

Sephie frowned. "You'll see." Leading him into the house and to the kitchen, she said, "We had that weird thing with the dishwasher." She reached for the knob on the laundry room door.

"Are the washer and dryer speaking in tongues, too?"

She shook her head. Opening the door, Sephie took a startled breath. Sitting perfectly upright, the jug of laundry detergent looked innocent, although a telltale dribble of blue goo decorated one side and a spot on the floor.

"Did something startle you and you dropped the soap?" Floyd asked.

Sephie pointed at the offending objective. "I was pulling dishes out of the cabinet. It fell and was on its side."

Studying the shelf, Floyd pronounced, "How could it fall with that barrier on the shelf?"

"That's what I'm saying," the old woman said. "It felt creepy in here so I just left it. There. On its side."

"Maybe Easter picked it up."

"No, I was with her every minute."

"Why would it right itself?" Floyd asked, looking at the jug before grabbing a dirty dishcloth from a pile of laundry on top of the washer and picking up the bottle.

"It wouldn't," Sephie argued. "But it sure didn't want the contents to spill all over the floor."

He wiped the jug and tightened the lid before putting it back on the shelf.

"Maybe that was Agnesia just wanting my attention," she said. "I have let the laundry pile up. She righted the jug because she always hated messes."

Motioning the old woman out of the room, Floyd quipped, "Then maybe she shouldn't have dropped the jug in the first place."

Near his head, the laundry products on the shelf trembled, rattling the wire construction holding them. Floyd gently pushed Sephie out into the kitchen and shut the door. "Yeah. I think that was your sister. Now, what about this other thing?"

Instead of going directly to the pantry, Sephie sat down on one of the kitchen chairs. Pointing to the pantry, she said, "There's a witch ball or a witch bullet in there."

"A what?" Floyd said walking over to the pantry door.

"Don't open that door! It'll get out."

"How're we supposed to get food to make dinner?"

"There's lunch meat," Sephie countered.

Giving her a very paternal look, he walked over to the table, pulled out a chair, and sat. "All right. Tell me about this witch bullet. What is it?"

Sephie started to get up, but Floyd waved her down. "What do you need?"

"I just need some water."

Floyd went to the fridge and pulled out a pitcher of brewed tea. "There's tea," he said. When she waved a hand at him, he asked, "So, what's a witch bullet?" He took two glasses from the cabinet and filled them with tea.

"Well, from what the old people used to say a witch bullet is a tiny version of a witch ball. They're made of hair."

Floyd put the glasses of tea on the table and went back to the counter for sugar and spoons. "Whose hair?"

"That's the thing. Depends on what the witch ball is used for."

Retrieving a small dish of sliced lemons from the fridge, Floyd finally sat down. "And what is that?"

Spooning sugar into her glass, Sephie mused. "I heard if you wanted to hex somebody's milk cow, you'd make the witch bullet from cow hair, anybody's cow. You'd make tiny pea sized witch balls and throw them or shoot them through a pea shooter at the cow."

"Why'd anyone want to do that?

"If you had an enemy, you'd make his cow go dry and not give any milk or taint the milk in some way. You tampered with his food or livelihood."

"Well, there's no cow here."

After adding lemon, Sephie tasted her tea. "No, and what's in the pantry's not pea sized. And it has a mind of its own."

"What's it look like?"

She made "C" shape with her right hand. "That big. Gray. Easter thought it was made from the witch's hair. But that wouldn't get to the one you wanted to hex. It had to be made from the hair of the hexed person."

"So, we have a tennis ball-sized wad of somebody's gray hair in the pantry," Floyd repeated calmly. He narrowed his eyes at Sephie's medium length gray hair.

The old woman pulled a section of her hair by her cheek and looked up. "Not mine. It would have taken weeks or months to gather that much."

"Agnesia's?"

She shrugged. "But who'd want to hex her? And why now? Besides it went after me."

Sipping his own tea, Floyd considered the seriousness of the situation. "So, how do we dispose of the thing?"

"We have to burn it."

He nodded. "I can make a fire out back."

"Catching it will be tricky. You can't let it touch you. It can either leave red welts where it hit you or it can penetrate your body. Either way, it'll do harm."

Rising, Floyd said, "Let's catch this thing first. Get me a plastic bowl or a colander or strainer."

Sephie went to a counter where she had pulled out items she didn't think she'd use and found a plastic colander with a handle.

Floyd opened the back door to a mud room and found a snow shovel. Joining Sephie, he leaned the shovel against the wall next to the pantry near the doorknob. Taking the plastic colander from her, he said, "Shut the door when I'm inside." Carefully, he opened the door and jerked on the cord of the light switch in the ceiling as Sephie closed the door but didn't shut it completely. Movement on the floor in a corner caught his eye. He slowly stalked forward. There was a flicker of movement before something dashed forward toward him. Slamming the colander over the object, Floyd reached a hand behind him. "The shovel."

Sephie immediately brought him the snow shovel. Floyd stooped and carefully tipped the colander a half inch, noticing that whatever was inside was bouncing back and forth against the sides of the plastic as if trying to find a way out. He lifted it a little more and slid the thin blade of the snow shovel under the colander. The surface area of the shovel was big enough to accommodate the colander and its contents. Straightening, Floyd carried the thing out of the pantry. Sephie hurried toward the back door and opened it for him.

Outside, he gently set his burden down. "Sephie, I need you to keep the colander over this thing."

Sephie took handle of the shovel from him, keeping the blade flat on the ground. Then she stooped to put her hand on the colander.

It didn't take Floyd long to build a small fire in a patch of dirt behind the house. When the blaze was hot enough, he took up Sephie's burden and moved everything closer to the fire. "Are their words you say?" he asked.

She shrugged. "Guess we make do."

"Then let me." Floyd chanted something and then used the colander to rake the object into the fire. It writhed and screamed in the flames only seconds before being totally consumed.

Resting on the shovel handle, Floyd looked at Sephie. "Life with you sure is different."

Chapter 18

Day 6: Saturday, Sephie's home,
Dark Hollow, TN, morning

Sitting on the edge of her bed, Sephie smiled as she watched Floyd button up another cotton shirt, even though she knew that the rest of her life would be spent ironing those shirts for him. He just wasn't a t-shirt kind of guy. She herself had donned a t-shirt and jeans and was struggling to tie her tennis shoes as she thought about today's tasks.

She planned on sorting the living room and her sitting room, the door to which Agnesia had always required that she keep shut. Her sister had never approved of books other than the Bible. And in truth, Sephie had some titles that would have made Agnesia start her own Farenheit 451 bonfire outside. Today, Sephie was going to pack up books to donate to the school library and the library in town. The more controversial titles she'd pack up for Mandy and Laura's shop, and she'd box up her own selections for her home with Floyd. She shook her head. She had never even seen where she'd live with him. She didn't even know if he had room for her books or any of her things.

When she stood, she turned to look at the old iron bedstead. It wasn't one of those ornate Victorian wrought iron works of beauty. This one was functional and old. It kept the mattress and box springs off the floor, just barely, sagging tiredly in the middle. Sephie was surprised the old thing hadn't broken down before now. Earl had bought it when they had first gotten married, and the old monstrosity had been transported in and out of tiny apartments until they had been able to buy the land on this ridge and build a house big enough for a family, even if it was just only one child.

"Memories?" Floyd asked coming to stand beside her.

"Some," she said. "It's a sad sight, isn't it?"

He put his arm around her as if unwilling to make a comment on someone else's marriage bed and the one they had been occupying.

Sephie squinted up at him. "It's not a comfortable bed. I bet your back tells you that every morning."

"We can pick out a new bed when we get home."

"What about yours?" she asked.

"That one does hurt my back." He pulled her closer to his side as he looked down at her. "A new bed. A fresh start." He leaned down to give her a long lingering kiss.

Something crashed onto the floor of the next room.

Slowly, Floyd raised his head and took a deep breath. "Miss Agnesia, I do have a right to kiss my own wife. Thank you very much."

Sephie whispered up at him. "But it's not official yet."

He looked at her a long time before he said, "In the eyes of my ancestors, it is, when you came to me with an open heart."

She frowned. "But others—"

"No!" he cut her off a little roughly. Then he repeated gently, "No. That was youth and need and maybe desperation. This. You." The fingers of his free hand brushed her cheek. "No." Then he kissed her once more as if she were something precious.

Sephie rested her hand on the crispness of his shirt as she moved ever so slightly away from him to look at the face that she welcomed seeing every morning across from a kitchen table, asking what she had planned for the day. She had never expected a Floyd in her life. "I don't doubt your intentions, old man. I never have. You just were so sure so early."

He smiled. "How could anyone not love you?"

84

That made her catch her breath, and she buried her face in the warmth of his shirt, allowing him to engulf her in his comforting energy and his protective arms.

Chapter 19

Day 6: Saturday, Sephie's home,
Dark Hollow, TN, late afternoon

The top sheet smelled of lavender fabric softener from the dryer as Sephie cast it into the air above the guest room bed. It fell gently into place so Sephie could fold the top into a crease and then make hospital corners on the bottom. She covered it with a quilt that had also had been freshly laundered. Straightening, she arched her back to relieve the ache from not just the bed making but the sorting and packing she'd done downstairs. She had dusted the room and opened a window to let in fresh air. The guest room hadn't been used in several years. Debra and Joe preferred to stay in a motel with a pool when they visited, usually in Lafollette or another larger town.

The house could use some young life in it. She was glad Floyd had invited James to stay with them and help them manage the packing and hauling. She did want to take the bureau from her room and some bookcases. But it would all depend on how much they could put in Floyd's truck. In any case, they could certainly use James' help.

The slam of vehicle doors drew Sephie to the window. Floyd was back with the young man. James carried his guitar case and another object the size of an old-fashioned, lady's cosmetic case. Floyd hoisted a duffle bag onto his shoulder before he led the boy in.

Sephie turned from the window to walk down the hall to greet them. At the top of the stairs, she called down, "Come and put your things in your room, James."

The young man hurried up the stairs with Floyd in his wake.

The old man stopped to give Sephie a paternal disapproving frown. Ignoring his silent admonition for her unnecessarily climbing stairs, Sephie led James to the guest room.

Putting his guitar and case down. James scanned the room. "This is so nice of you, Miz Sephie."

"Our pleasure. The bathroom is next door at the end of the hall. Our room is opposite yours. I hope you can sleep well here." Then she bit her lower lip, looking at Floyd, wondering whether to tell James about Agnesia's tantrums in the house.

"I'm sure I will. But if I don't, I'll just get up and play for a bit. I don't have to plug in the amp."

"Amp? Is it out in the truck?" Sephie was thinking of the ones she's seen before on small stages that were the size of a Pullman bag.

James pointed to the little box beside his guitar case. "It's a practice amp, but still can fill a small room like Connie's. And it's loud enough for church."

"Speaking of which," Floyd said. "I can give you a ride to the services that you play at tomorrow."

"That would be great. I have a 9:30 service at Trinity Baptist and an 11:00 at Grace Methodist. I'll need to tell them both I'll be leaving soon."

"Hopefully, we can get what we need to get done here taken care of quickly. You must be eager to get home," Sephie said.

"Yes, I am, but. . . ."

"But?" Floyd prompted.

"I've been gone a long time."

"Family never forgets."

Sitting down on the edge of the bed, he confessed. "I didn't leave with my family's blessing."

"It won't matter," Floyd said.

"Why don't you give them a call and tell them you're coming home," Sephie suggested.

"I don't know if I remember their number."

"Everybody puts those numbers into their phones," Sephie said. "I doubt anybody remembers anybody's numbers anymore. I've gotten lazy myself, relying on those things."

Floyd stepped to James and gave him a firm pat on the back. "After supper, we can make some calls together. We'll find them." He turned to Sephie. "And you, young lady, we need to talk" he said, putting his arm around her.

"About supper? I was thinking of making pork chops."

Propelling her out of the room and out of James' earshot, he said, "I don't want you taking the stairs by yourself again."

"Oh lordy, Floyd, I take them slow, and I stop when it hurts too much."

"Up and down once a day is more than enough."

"I had to make up his bed."

"And?"

"I changed our sheets, too."

"And?"

"Washed all of the towels and put them away."

Shaking his head. "So, several times up and down. Sephie, when we get home, I'm taking you to Bismarck to an orthopedic surgeon and arrange for a hip replacement before the wedding."

"You expecting me to get frisky afterwards then?"

Floyd just shook his head. "Old woman, get your mind back on supper. Pork chops sound good. Let me do them. You do the sides."

As Floyd patiently steadied her as she slowly went down the stairs, Sephie asked, "Should we tell James about Agnesia?"

"Let's just wait and see how your sister reacts to him being in the house."

When they got to the bottom of the stairs, Floyd asked, "Did the washing machine speak in tongues, too, today?"

Sephie shook her head. "No. Everything ran normally. But then I didn't stay and listen. I was busy packing books. I made a good dint into the lot." In the kitchen, Sephie went to the pantry for potatoes and a quart of turnip and mustard greens. "Will there be room for a couple of bookcases at your house? I want to take some of my books."

Pulling pork chops from the fridge that Sephie had evidently pulled out to thaw, Floyd said, "We can build a bookcase in every room if you want."

Sephie put her food down and found a paring knife in a drawer. "You're going to get tired of trying to please me all the time."

"Never," he said.

Easing herself into a chair, she started peeling potatoes. "Well, I'm not used to it."

"That's why I won't stop," Floyd said, pulling out spices to season the pork chops.

Sephie shook her head and laughed. "Old man, what am I going to do with you?"

"Just stay and put up with me."

Chapter 20

Day 6: Saturday, Sephie's home,
Dark Hollow, TN, early evening

The quiet twang of a metal slide over strings drifted down from upstairs. Sephie paused at the stove, lifting the potato masher from the pot before adding milk. She listened, trying to fit the notes to a tune. Recognizing it, she hummed along, putting in a generous tablespoon of butter and a splash of milk, finally singing the words of "Mansion on the Hilltop" as she beat the potatoes with a wooden spoon.

Floyd turned the pork chops in the iron skillet and hummed along. "That's one I don't know," he said.

"It's probably for the Baptist Church," Sephie said. "I wonder what he'll do for the Methodists."

"I think I'll recognize those," Floyd said, putting the pork chops onto a platter. "We used a Methodist hymnal when we first started the choir back home because the shipment of Catholic hymnals had somehow gotten sent to Pine Ridge instead of Fort Berthold. We liked those hymns so much, we kept singing them." He put the platter on the table as Sephie dished up the mashed potatoes into a big bowl. The greens had already been put out.

"Maybe we should go to the Methodist service with James tomorrow," Floyd suggested.

As Sephie placed the bowl in the middle of the well-laid table, she said, "I think I'd like that. It'd feel good to do some singing with some instruments and where I didn't have to worry about snakes getting loose."

Floyd chuckled. "I'll go call James."

The old man had barely left the kitchen when a loud crash reverberated throughout the house. Sephie hurriedly followed Floyd to the foot of the stairs. As he started up, James came running down the hall, stopping at the top, looking frightened out of his wits.

"What was that?" he demanded.

Calmly, Floyd said, "Let's find out."

Sephie started up the stairs behind him.

Hearing her, Floyd turned. "Stay down there, Sephie."

"Not this time," she said. "I want to see what happened."

Floyd waited for her, and all three went down the hall to Agnesia's room. The bureau was still on the floor from this morning. Floyd and Sephie had agreed to just leave it there. The bed, however, looked as if it had been lifted and slammed down again or somehow pulled about three feet away from the wall it had abutted. A ginger jar lamp on the nightstand had crashed to the floor; its porcelain remains spilling onto the linoleum.

Sephie frowned. She wasn't upset by the loss of a lamp that she'd bought when she'd first gotten married. She was angry at her sister for trying to scare their houseguest. Before she could stop herself, she shook her fist and yelled, "Agnesia, you stop this nonsense right now! You've no right frightening our guest! And it was a hymn, for gosh sakes!"

She turned to Floyd, seeking his reaction, when she saw the look on James' face.

"You've got an *i da hi*?" James asked.

Floyd frowned and then said, "A *dok i da hi*. Yes. It isn't a *mahopamiis*, a bad witch."

"Who then?"

"My sister," Sephie said, "A very devout Christian woman."

"Did she die here?"

Sephie shook her head. "I was told she was taken to the hospital and died there."

James nodded repeatedly.

"She doesn't approve of Floyd and me," Sephie admitted. "She probably doesn't approve of your music. She was a Primitive Baptist."

"What?" James searched Floyd's face for an explanation.

"They sing but don't use instruments," the old man explained.

"How long are you planning on staying here?" James asked.

"We'll leave as soon as we're packed up," Floyd said.

"I thought it might be a month," Sephie said. "But I just want to get my things packed up and then we'll go. It might only be a week if we all pitch in. I'm selling all the furniture."

James stared at the broken lamp. "Is this her house?"

"No," Sephie said. "It's mine. But she lived here with me for ten years. The kitchen really is where she spent most of her time."

The young man raised his head. "And that's where we eat?"

Floyd put his hand on James' shoulder. "She hasn't bothered us there. C'mon, dinner's ready."

Chapter 21

Day 7: Sunday, Grace Methodist Church,
Dark Hollow, TN, noon

Holding on to Floyd's arm, Sephie steadied herself as she navigated down the concrete steps outside of Grace Methodist Church.

"Did you like the service?" Floyd asked.

"Yes, I did," Sephie said honestly. "Good singing. A sensible sermon. No drama. I was glad to put my $5 into the collection plate. I really liked James's playing, too."

"They have a good little band there, which surprised me." Finally reaching the sidewalk, he looked up at the red brick church with its white pillars flanking the double front doors. "I expected a lot of organ music."

"When I went to the restroom, I heard one of the ladies say that they have two services. A more traditional one earlier in the morning and this one later with drums and electric guitars. They said that more young people came to this one, and they sure did. I was surprised to see so many teenagers."

"Well, they did do upbeat rock arrangements of a couple of old hymns that got the kids up singing. And those two songs from *Godspell*."

"Wasn't that a play? They seemed familiar."

"Yep, back in the 70s. We've borrowed a few from that show for some special events and one or two from *Jesus Christ Superstar* during Lent. It was effective to use 'Prepare Ye the Way of the Lord" as a call to worship and "Day by Day" as a prelude to communion."

"Didn't they do a song from that play B.D. was in, the one about Huck Finn?"

95

Floyd chuckled. "That was another clever choice, using ""Waiting for the Light to Shine" after the children's moment."

Sephie sighed. "B.D. would've loved that service."

"When we get back, I think I might pull music for a special service and bring B.D. in to sing. I know I'm going to rope James into playing for us. We just might get more young people to come, too." He patted Sephie's hand. "I'm going to put him in charge of music for our wedding ceremonies."

Sephie jerked her head up. "Plural?"

"Of course, a traditional one and one in the church. I'm hoping James can round up drummers and singers. It'll be good for him to seek those traditional players and reconnect with his spiritual side. He can also pull together a band for the church and reception."

"You got this all planned out, don't you? What if I just want someone from the courthouse to marry us?"

"That's what I did and Mandy and Laura did. Do you really want that?"

She shook her head. "I was married in a church, but we couldn't afford much. I made a simple dress and wore a big white hat. One of my friends made us a cake, and we had the reception in my daddy's home. He was a widower by then."

"Would you like a real wedding gown this time?'

Sephie grunted. "What would I do with something like that now? Besides I'm not a virginal bride anymore, and I have no one to pass the dress down to."

Floyd covered her hand with his. "I bet there's a young girl still inside you that would want one. You could give the dress to a young bride who couldn't afford a dress."

As they neared the truck, Sephie asked, "And how are we going to pay for two weddings and a reception? And pay for a hip replacement? Lordy, I wanted us to live on the sale of the house. We deserve an easier life."

Floyd smiled. "Trust Spirit."

Chapter 22

The smell of cooked chicken filled the kitchen, drawing Sephie, Floyd, and James toward the room.

"I thought Agnesia didn't have modern appliances," Floyd said noticing the crockpot on the counter and heading to a stack of dishes nearby.

"She didn't," Sephie said, putting on an apron. "I found all mine in the back of a cabinet. I put the chicken and the vegetables in my crockpot when you took James to his first service this morning. I think I timed this just about right. There should be some leftover biscuits from breakfast."

"That sure smells good," James said, taking three plates from Floyd and setting the table.

The old man followed behind with silverware and a plastic bag of biscuits.

"I knew we'd be hungry when we got home." Sephie found a platter. With a big carving fork stuck in the breast and a slotted spoon inserted inside the cavity, she carefully removed the chicken from the crockpot, tipping the bird slightly to let the cooking juices flow out. Once the bird was on the platter, she sifted out the carrots, celery, and potatoes. Then she spooned out a few of the onions she'd placed on the bottom of the pot.

When the old woman started to lift the heavy platter, James intercepted her actions. "It looks heavy, ma'am."

Sephie let him take it to the table. "Y'all gotta start calling me something besides ma'am, son." She looked at Floyd. "If he's supposed to be your distant cousin, shouldn't he be mine, too?"

97

"Like Mandy is my great-niece now?" he responded, raising an eyebrow.

She nodded.

"That's not how it works," James said.

Sephie eased herself into a chair and started to dismember the bird with a knife. "Oh" was all she could say. But in her mind, she thought *I guess I'll always be that old White woman who doesn't know the rules*. Her throat caught on that reality, but she kept separating drumsticks and thighs from the bird. She never realized that a life with Floyd wouldn't be like the one she had had with her late husband. Their two families recognized that they had gained new relatives. Whether individuals liked each other or not, they tolerated everyone because they were family. Attacking the white meat, Sephie cut a few slices and then put the carving knife and fork down, suddenly losing her appetite.

She pushed the platter closer to James. "Help yourself," she said, getting up. She went to the fridge and pulled out a pitcher of lemonade. Finding three glasses on the counter, she started filling them. Coming back to the table with two, she placed them in front of James and Floyd who had filled their plates. By the time she sat down again with her own glass of lemonade, she could only stare at her empty plate.

What was she doing? She was leaving all that she ever had known to do what? Start a life with someone she hardly knew and live in a culture she would never be a part of. But what did she really have here? A crazy cousin or two and Lige's moonshine? She didn't even have a home church. Agnesia at least had work at hers and the respect of all those church ladies.

Getting up from the table, Sephie left the men and went through the living room to the porch outside. She leaned on the wooden railing, taking in the woods around her. Beyond that, the old woman saw the clear cut on the far mountain. This wasn't strip mining or logging that she'd seen more and more of since her husband had passed. She noticed movement over there. Trucks and heavy equipment crept up and down the mountain, dropping off loads and going for more. Something very large was being built there, not just a big house or even a hotel. It looked as if there would be a whole village of buildings. It would probably be a new resort or one of those gated communities with a clubhouse, a pool, and a golf course. In a few short years, she wouldn't be able to see the wilderness she had viewed from that porch for over fifty years. It was time to go. If she stayed, it would break her heart.

She sighed. If she left, she would have to learn how to navigate another culture and accept that she would always be an outsider. Maybe she had always been one even in her own family and she definitely was in Earl's. Still, she'd have to get used to those awful North Dakota winters Mandy told her about.

A warm hand at her waist made her jump.

"It's only me," Floyd said quietly, turning her toward him so that he could wrap her in his arms. "What troubles you?"

Placing her hands on his shirt, she admitted, "Change." She swallowed. "It's hard. At this age." She paused. "Having to learn new ways to live." She swallowed again as her throat tightened. "Wondering if I belong."

"Is this because of what James said?"

She hesitated before admitting, "I hadn't considered what this would all mean."

"Claiming kin is a matter of blood or marriage. James can be my cousin but you have no ties to him, except through me. He will always be your husband's cousin. Just like Mandy will always by your great-niece but not mine." He smiled at her. "We're very different people, Sephie, but we add value to each other's lives. My people will love you. Yolanda does. You just have to give them time to get to know you."

She offered him a small, conciliatory smile.

A loud crash and a yelp made them both jump.

Rushing inside to the kitchen, they found James backed up against the far cabinets. His gaze was cemented onto the mess on the floor near the counter by the stove. The crockpot lay on its side, spilling thick chicken broth all over the linoleum.

Sephie stared at the mess, her eyes welling with tears. She was furious. "Agnesia, you stop this right this minute! You can throw your own furniture around and even break my lamp, but when you start breaking my cookware and wasting food, that's the last straw! And you're frightening the boy! I'm bringing in a priest. See how you like that!"

The old woman picked up the crockpot and set it back on the counter. By sheer luck the inner crockery looked intact, but only a good washing would find out if it had a crack in it. The outer heating element was badly bent. Sephie wasn't sure she should even try turning it on.

When she turned to deal with the chicken broth on the floor, Floyd already was applying a mop to the mess and wringing it out into a bucket.

"That would have made some good soup tomorrow," Sephie said. Remembering James, she walked over to him.

"That-that was your sister?" he stammered.

"Guess so," Sephie said, putting a calming hand on the young man's rolled up sleeve.

Removing his gaze from Floyd's ministrations, he searched Sephie's face. "Are you really going to bring in a priest?"

"I may need to," she said.

"They won't do an exorcism," Floyd said.

"We don't need one," Sephie said. "We just need a blessing."

"Maybe we should ask her pastor," he suggested. "She might listen to him."

"Those folks believe in a lot of things, but I don't know if they believe in haints, especially one who was supposed to be on an express train to heaven."

"Aren't there conjure doctors who could do more?" James asked.

"Conjure doctors?" Sephie echoed. "You sound like B.D. He knows who to call in his bayou country. But I never heard of any conjure doctors here. I don't know of any faith healers or even Grannies who know how to deal with spirits."

"I heard somebody talk about some kind of conjure or hex doctor who did."

"At the bar and grill?" Floyd asked.

"Yeah. I could call over there and see if anybody remembers," James suggested.

Hauling the bucket of broth toward the back door, Floyd said, "It might be worth looking into. Sephie, maybe one of those crazy cousins of yours knows somebody."

The old woman thought about that while Floyd tossed the broth far into the woods and came back in to put all-purpose cleaner into the bucket with water from the sink. As he applied himself to the floor, Sephie placed an arm around James and urged him back to the table. "You should finish your dinner."

"You need to eat, too," James said.

The old woman smiled and nodded, pulling her plate across the table to sit beside him. She didn't want to get in Floyd's way while he worked. The old woman served herself from the platter. "I've lived in this house for over 50 years. It's always been a quiet place, even when my daughter was small and she'd bring in her giggling little friends."

"Is your sister upset that I'm here?"

Sephie grunted. "She's been upset about Floyd and me. We aren't official yet."

"That matters to her?"

"Guess so." Tasting a bite of chicken, she realized she was hungry. "She's been trying to pray me into heaven for the past ten years."

"Why?"

Sephie laughed. "Because I'm not her, I guess. I feel more Spirit in the woods than I do in a building, especially one that doesn't have good music. Oh, the singing is good, but they don't even have a piano. I do enjoy a good hymn sing." She attacked the vegetables, enjoying the flavor the chicken broth had given them. "I really liked the music at the Methodist church this morning."

"I enjoy playing for them. They always test the boundaries there. It's working by getting more teenagers at those services."

"How'd they find out about you?"

"The music director was having dinner with some choir members and he heard me play."

"At Connie's?"

He nodded.

Sephie chuckled. "That's right. Methodists tipple a little."

"Nothing wrong with a glass of something with a meal."

Remembering Cousin Lige's butterscotch moonshine in the pantry, Sephie nearly whispered. "I have a little something for after dinner, but we'd better take it out on the porch." She nodded her head upward, indicating Agnesia.

Floyd looked up as he reached down for the bucket. "Somebody make a delivery while I was gone?"

"Cousin Easter brought it. She hid it in the pantry. T. Berry still considers himself law enforcement."

"Illegal wh—" James started to say as Sephie grabbed his arm and put her finger over her lips.

"Butterscotch," she said.

"Your cousin making flavored now?" Floyd said, carting the bucket and mop toward the powder room on the first floor.

"Seems to be the new thing. Like your honey one."

"It might ease your bones," the old man said.

"I take it your sister wouldn't approve," James speculated.

"I'm going to hell."

Chapter 23

Day 8: Monday, deep in Dark Hollow, TN, afternoon

The fat old man released the screen door to let it slam loudly on the porch of an old two-story farmhouse. Emitting a deep laugh, he scratched the neckline of his white t-shirt where blond and gray chest hairs protruded and stepped down the two steps to the hard-packed dirt yard to meet his visitors. As he moved, he tested the stitching of the overalls stretched tightly across his protruding belly.

Sephie slid out of the truck to land a little too hard onto the ground, causing her to wince and release a soft cry of discomfort.

Floyd appeared at her elbow immediately, moving her a step or two away to close her door.

"Well now, cousin," the portly man greeted Sephie, opening his arms wide. "I never thought I'd see you show up so boldly in my yard."

Sephie stepped into the welcoming arms for a brief hug. "I'm surprising myself in my old age, Lige."

Stepping away from her to extend his hand to Floyd. "I can see that. I'd heard you'd found yourself a man."

"Floyd Whiteman," the old man said as he shook hands.

Lige laughed. "You sure ain't that."

"I had a Welsh ancestor whose name nobody could pronounce."

"Welsh?" the portly man looked at Sephie. "He might be kin, you know." Turning back to Floyd, he said, "I'm Lige Smith. The folks at Ellis Island didn't even try to spell my

Welsh ancestor's name." Crossing his burly arms across his belly, he asked, "What nation?"

Floyd raised an eyebrow. "Mandan/Hidatsa."

"That's not one around here."

"Fort Berthold, North Dakota."

Lige nodded.

"You know the local nations here?" Floyd asked.

"Been looking into my forefathers—" He chuckled. "And foremothers. There was a family story about one grandmother way back."

"Did you find her?"

Lige laughed. "Lord no! Everybody around these parts thinks they have that one Indian that makes them pure blood or something. When I was growin' up, you wanted to hide that sort of connection but not now. My grandson's been educatin' me on it."

"Who? Richard?" Sephie asked.

"Naw. Richard's got his head so far up his butt in video games he don't know what day it is."

"He's what? In his second year at East Tennessee State?"

"Third. A waste of a good education, if you ask me. He thinks he's going to make a killing thinking up a new game." Motioning them to the porch, he said, "Come sit a spell."

Sephie followed and settled herself carefully onto a wooden porch swing as Floyd steadied it for her and then seated himself. "If not Richard, then who?"

"Pollard," Lige grunted, easing himself into the plastic weave of a patio rocker.

"Pollard? What got him interested in family history?"

Lige laughed again. "A girl. What else?"

"This girl's interested in our family?"

"Not particularly. She just wants Pollard to know all about his."

"Why? Where'd he meet her?"

"Up at the college. Richard lured him up there for some party. Took him away from a good paying job with Pete Ferguson at his plumbing business for three whole days. He's been expanding and Pollard's been learning the trade from him. The girl was up there, talking to some professors. Her people are tryin' to get recognized by the state."

"Her people?" Floyd interrupted.

"Yep. They got a funny name. The Yuchi or to be correct: the Remnant Yuchi. Only tribe around here that calls itself a nation other than the Cherokee."

"Yuchi," Floyd repeated slowly.

"Ever hear of it?" Sephie asked.

Floyd slowly shook his head. "But there're all sorts of nations out there that I've never come across." He turned to Lige. "So, she wants your grandson to know his roots?"

Nodding, the fat man just said, "Yep." Then he stretched his bulk forward as if to hoist himself up. "Y'all want a sip o' something?"

"We got plenty at home, thank you," Sephie said. "That butterscotch sure is different."

"Different?" Lige settled back, chuckling. "Guess it is. Y'all like it?"

Sephie nodded. "Too much. I need to keep that hidden some place."

Her cousin paused, looking them both over. "Now, what brings y'all to my doorstep if not for my handiwork?"

"Well," Sephie began. "We've been experiencing some strange things at the house."

"Like what? Agnesia come back as a haint?"

Sephie glanced at Floyd uncomfortably and then back at Lige.

"She didn't!" The fat man boomed out and leaned forward. "What's she doin'?"

"Tipping furniture mainly, breaking a few things."

"Y'all know why?"

Sephie was silent. Floyd jumped into the gap and admitted. "I don't think she likes me. Us."

Lige laughed again. "Y'all ain't official yet, huh?"

"We'll get married later after I get settled in North Dakota," Sephie admitted. "You'd think that wouldn't matter at our age."

"North Dakota! Now, I do need a drink! How're you gonna survive up there in the frozen North?" His gaze fell on Floyd, and he started laughing. "Oh, yeah. I see." Turning back to his cousin, he said, "So, what're you gonna do about Agnesia?"

"Nothing," Sephie said. "I just hope she stays here or settles down a bit. If I have to, I'll get someone to help me nudge her on into the afterlife — if I can find somebody."

"You mean a haint doctor? Ain't seen one of them round here since I was a kid. Mother called one in after Granny passed. She died hard and didn't want to leave."

"I'll probably need to beat the bushes to find one then. What about somebody who can stop a witch sending?"

"A witch — what y'all got yourself into, Sephie? You piss somebody off?"

"Not me! Agnesia must've took great joy in pissing people off other than me."

"You seen something? Or get a gift?"

"If you can call it a gift."

"What?"

Sephie was reluctant to answer and Floyd didn't jump in to help out.

"Out with it," Lige insisted.

"A witch ball."

Lige whistled.

"The thing was rolling around my kitchen with a mind of its own. I got Floyd to take the dang thing out and burn it."

Lige nodded. "Wise thing to do. Y'all don't want one of them to stay long in your house." He looked over at Floyd.

"Y'all didn't let it touch you, did ya?"

"No, I was careful," Floyd said.

Lige thought for a while. "Them things don't show up for no reason. Anything else happen that ain't Agnesia."

Sephie really didn't want to talk about the dishwasher. "Mostly it's been Agnesia and the witch ball."

"And the dishwasher," Floyd said. "I heard it myself."

Leaning forward again, Lige asked, "What was it doing?"

"Speaking in tongues, if you must know," Sephie admitted.

"Say what?" Lige searched Floyd's face as if he was the voice of reason.

The old man shrugged. "It was strange. But I've never heard many people speak in tongues before."

"It was tongues!" Sephie insisted. "But in a growly kind of voice. Or it was a demon."

Lige chuckled. "So, your dishwasher is possessed. That's a new one on me."

"I don't know about that," Floyd said. "It only happened one time."

"It stopped after I salted the thing," Sephie said. "So, do you know anybody who can help us? I just need some protections until we leave in a few days. I don't want to take anything with me."

"Sounds like you need a preacher, and me and preachers give each other a wide berth."

"I don't think a preacher or even—" Sephie glanced at Floyd. "—a priest would even come to help. I don't think they believe in any of that stuff today. And certainly not about things. People — maybe they'd come out to pray."

Lige rocked a minute in thought. Finally, he pursed his lips together and then nodded. "Y'all might ask Pollard's girl."

"East Tennessee State's is a ways away, right?" Sephie asked.

"Johnson City. About a two-three hour drive."

She sighed and looked at Floyd. "Guess we got to make a trip. But we'd better get Pollard to call her and tell us where to find her."

Lige chuckled. "Y'all don't have to go that far. She's right here in Dark Holler working in the drug store."

Chapter 24

Day 8: Monday, Dark Hollow, TN, late afternoon

As Sephie stepped through the open door that Floyd held for her at the entrance of Duncan's Home Town Pharmacy, he teased, "Smith, huh? Bet your folks got looks when they registered at motels."

Sephie frowned at him. "A plain name. Maybe that's why we all had really unusual first names. But it sure isn't helping Lige any with tracing our ancestors. Just how many real Smiths do you think there are out there and not aliases?"

"Well, Smith describes a trade. There are all sorts of trades: blacksmith, silversmith, goldsmith, swordsmith, gunsmith, locksmith, even coopersmith. Those all deal with metals of some kind."

"Except coopersmith. Isn't that a barrel maker?"

"I think so. But your name, like mine, deals with people who couldn't pronounce or write our Welsh ancestors' names. I don't know how Lige will ever find who that ancestor was. There's no record of mine."

Inside the cool drug store, Sephie and Floyd separated to make quick work of their search for Pollard's girlfriend. The old woman immediately scanned who was at the register where an older woman manned the till. She then walked to the cosmetic counter and found a young blond woman applying an X-acto knife to a box. Sephie examined the clerk's features as she started pulling out bottles of nail polish and setting them on the glass display case. Seeing that the clerk didn't seem to be native, Sephie moved the other side of the store to the photo section. There she found a young man completing a transaction with a middle-aged woman.

"There you are," Floyd said as she turned to begin an aisle-by-aisle search for a stocking clerk who might be the young native woman they were looking for. "I found her. We've been having a nice conversation."

"You did? Where?"

"She's the pharmacist. Didn't you think she could be?" he asked as he led her toward the other side of the store.

"I didn't think she'd have a career. That's no reflection on her. Pollard just doesn't have aspirations and his past girlfriends weren't very bright."

"Maybe she's been a good influence."

A pretty young woman in a white lab coat joked with an elderly couple as she handed them a white paper bag that probably held their medications. Her shiny black hair was kept off her face in one long braid that fell almost to her waist. Her smile was not only kind but reflected a sensitivity of spirit that produced a smile on Sephie's face. But it was her eyes when she turned to Floyd and then to Sephie after the other couple had walked away that caused the old woman to catch her breath in surprise. The girl projected the same warmth that Floyd had when she'd first met him, except this was turned to a higher wattage that assaulted her. Sephie swayed slightly, grabbing Floyd's arm to steady herself.

The young woman's face changed to concern as Floyd quickly guided Sephie to a nearby chair where customers could wait for prescriptions. The pharmacist disappeared only to return with a small bottle of water that she uncapped for the old woman. Squatting in front of Sephie, she asked, "Do you feel faint or dizzy?"

Sephie drank the cold liquid and just stared into the young woman's face, only then letting her gaze rest on the name badge she wore: Corinna Watson. Finally, Sephie looked up at Floyd. "She has powerful energy."

Floyd chuckled. "Yes, she does. But I didn't expect it to hit you like that."

"It's like yours. As a young man, you— Women had no chance around you."

Corinna opened her mouth in surprise while Floyd looked down embarrassed.

Sephie's attention returned to the girl. "And Pollard never knew what hit him."

"Pollard? You know Pollard?" She looked from Sephie to Floyd.

"He's my cousin's grandson," the old woman said. "However you count kin, he's some kind of cousin, I guess."

The young woman stood, slightly suspicious now. "Did you come to check up on who he's associating with?"

Sephie frowned, wondering at her sudden change of demeanor.

"Have you had trouble like that before?" Floyd asked.

"We aren't always welcome. And that family—" She stopped abruptly, looking up at Floyd. She lowered her eyes immediately.

"That family," Sephie repeated. "You mean my family. What have they been doing to you? Cousin Lige, Pollard's grandfather, seems to like you."

"He can't piss people off. It isn't good for business."

Sephie raised an eyebrow. "You use his wares?"

Corinna scanned the space around them as if to make sure no one overheard. She nodded. "I put up tinctures with it."

Smiling, Sephie leaned toward Corinna and almost whispered, "So do I. We should talk remedies sometime."

"So, the rest of the family has been intolerant?" Floyd asked.

Staring at Sephie, Corinna didn't speak for a long time. "It's the women."

Sephie flashed her eyes wide. "Don't look at me. You see who I'm with. I'm going to marry him."

Tightening her jaw, she finally admitted, "Just one who's been whipping up the church ladies in the community."

Narrowing her eyes, Sephie connected the dots. "Agnesia," she spat out, her anger growing.

Corinna nodded.

"Have I been living under a rock? I thought she had a personal crusade against me and not anybody else."

Floyd intervened. "It seems like we all have a lot to talk about. And not here. We actually came to ask for your help, for some knowledge you might have. Could we buy you dinner later? Not here in town, maybe over the state line at Connie's Café. You know it?"

Corinna nodded.

"I assure you our intentions are just for information about herbs and rites," Floyd said.

Glancing back down at Sephie, Corinna frowned. Seeming to come to a decision, she finally said, "I can meet you up at Connie's at 7. I'll get my intern to finish my shift."

Chapter 25

Day 8: Monday, Connie's Bar and Grill,
East Hollow Gap, KY, early evening

With the wailing sounds of another female country singer pining for her whiskey-drinking philandering husband in the background, Floyd, Sephie, and James concentrated on their menus in a booth in a far corner of Connie's. Fidgeting, the old woman twisted her body to look at the clock over the bar. "It's 7:30, do you think that girl stood us up?" she asked.

"It's only ten after 7," James said.

"But the clock—"

"Connie puts it ahead 20 minutes so she can get all of the patrons out before 2. They've been fined before for serving after closing."

"Don't the patrons complain?" Sephie asked.

James shrugged. "They all know about it so they come early to drink longer."

Floyd chuckled. "Can't keep some people away."

"But the girl's still late," Sephie complained.

"Maybe it took her longer to get ready," James offered.

"What's there to get ready for?" Sephie countered. "All she had to do was take off her white coat and get in her car. I think she doesn't want to help us because of my family."

James put his menu down. "What's this all about anyway?"

Floyd followed suit to give James his full attention. "Bigotry." He turned to Sephie, "I'm surprised they let me in the church for the funeral."

"Well, my family stayed away. But, knowing what Agnesia has been fanning, I'm surprised myself."

James frowned as he stared at Sephie and then Floyd. "Bigotry against us, native people," he said, finally figuring out their meaning. "So, this girl's native, too?"

At that moment, Floyd looked up. He rose from the booth and raised a hand toward the front of the café.

James twisted around the end of the booth and saw the young woman approaching. He, too, rose to offer her a seat on the bench he sat on.

Corinna Watson's face looked worried even as she noticed the two men were native. She was wearing jeans and a red blouse with a small string of beads around her neck.

Floyd offered his hand to shake. "Thank you for coming."

Corinna did so reluctantly and nodded at Sephie. "Ma'am."

James was noticeably silent, only motioning for her to sit on the bench.

She slid in, eying everyone warily. James perched himself on the very edge of the bench as if ready to flee at the least provocation.

Sephie normally would have tried to make small talk to make the girl feel more comfortable, but she herself wasn't feeling at ease.

Millie, their server from a few days ago, appeared at their table. "Oh lawdy, that new girl didn't leave y'all enough menus."

Pushing his menu toward Corinna, James said, "I'd take the cook's special. What's he doing tonight?"

"He's making fried rabbit."

"Where'd he get that?" Sephie asked.

Millie laughed. "He and his brother went out after closing and went shooting in Old Man Taylor's fallow field last night. He's been complaining about all the rabbits eating up his garden. So, the boys took their jeep and went hunting with pistols. Got 'em a dozen. And no buckshot in any of 'em."

"I haven't had rabbit since I was a child," Sephie said. "Does he parboil it and then dip it in buttermilk and bread it before he fries it?"

"Sure does."

"Then I'll take some."

"I'll have that, too," Floyd said. "I've never had it that way. My people just roasted it."

"Well, y'all got here early before it's all gone." Turning to Corinna, she said, "And what about you, hun?"

"Sure," Corinna said, without enthusiasm.

"It comes with mashed potatoes and sliced tomatoes. Anything to drink?"

"I'll have unsweetened iced tea," Floyd said, nodding to Sephie, "and she'll have a Jameson on the rocks."

Sephie batted his arm. "I can speak for myself, old man. Ever since I said yes, you been bossing me around."

"It'll help your bones, old woman. You aren't lacing your lemonade with a little something anymore."

"I still can't willingly bring liquor into that house after all my sister's squawking."

"But—" James began and stopped when Floyd gave him a fatherly look.

Turning back to Sephie, he added, "You just stashed it down at the cabin along with your tincture base."

"We needn't air our quarrels in public," Sephie said. She pursed her lips and frowned at Floyd, and then looked up at Millie. "Bring me an unsweetened iced tea with lemon." She paused. "Along with the Jameson."

Millie chuckled, turning to James, "Connie's got a new harvest ale. Want that?"

He nodded.

"And you, hon?"

Corinna looked at the faces around the booth as if she were weighing whether to order a drink or not. Finally, she sighed and reached into her purse for her wallet. Pulling out her ID, she offered it to Millie, who glanced at it, and then said, "I'll have a white wine, please."

Millie gathered up the menus and then put her hand on James' shoulder. "Sure miss you hanging round here. You still gonna play Friday night?"

"I'll be here."

She patted his shoulder and sashayed off to the kitchen.

In the silence that followed, Corinna asked, "Play?"

Floyd answered for James. "He plays blues guitar here on Friday nights. He's good."

She opened her mouth in a bit of surprise in recognition. "I may have heard you. But you play with that big black hat on and you're all bent over your guitar. Nobody sees your face."

Shyly, he offered his hand. "My name's James Redman."

She shook it with the first glimpse of enthusiasm she had displayed that evening.

"I'm sorry," Floyd said, "We never really introduced ourselves. I'm Floyd Whiteman, and this is Sephie soon to be Sephie Whiteman. James and I are some kind of long down-the-line cousins. He's Hidatsa and I'm Mandan/Hidatsa. I've got some Welsh in my background."

Corinna looked at Sephie. "You're a Smith." The surname she uttered came out as a curse.

Sephie nodded. "Smith and married a Hill. I'm a widow."

"And, James," Floyd began, "she's Corinna Watson. She's Remnant Yuchi. Did I get that right?"

She nodded and then turned to James. "You don't get flack for playing here?"

"Why would I?" he said. "I'm an entertainer. Nobody cares who you are on stage. Connie and her staff are good people. And with a name like Redman, people know who I am."

"So, was Agnesia upset you were dating Pollard, Cousin Lige's grandson?" Sephie asked, noticing the hopeful expression on James' face sag a bit after her announcement. "Was that her issue with you?"

"Pollard?" Corinna laughed then. "We aren't dating. I've just been helping him and his grandfather with genealogy. That boy doesn't know one end of a computer from another even though his brother is a hacker."

"A hacker?" Sephie squawked.

"That's a long story for another time. I don't even think Agnesia even knows who Pollard is really. That part of your family doesn't mingle too much with the others because of the grandfather's business."

Sephie leaned across the table toward James. "So, you know he makes shine," she said in a loud stage whisper. Straightening, she asked the young woman, "So, what set Agnesia's bonnet on fire then?"

Millie returned with drinks and then left. After they had all taken sips of their beverages, Corrina explained. "She saw me in the pharmacy. That made her uncomfortable. Then she'd heard that I'd helped a relative of one of the ladies at her church and that got her going."

"How'd you help her?" Sephie asked.

Corinna paused and then confessed. "I made an herbal tea for the old woman. I sang over it and told her to say a charm. The old woman didn't seem to be upset with that, as if she'd seen things like that before. But your sister—"

Sephie leaned back into the plastic upholstered booth back. "Oh lordy. That's what Agnesia has been trying to pray me into heaven for all these years. Your ways are different from mine, but they're the same to people like Agnesia. They all think it's from the Devil or worse."

"Some of those church people have some pretty strange ideas," James said. "I saw some weird things playing at that rival."

"Weirder than snake handling?" Floyd asked.

"Oh yeah. Casting out demons. And a lot of other stuff that'd make your hair stand up."

"Church isn't all bad," Floyd said. "Those Methodists have a good service, and I try to get some good singing out of the choir at Our Lady of the Plains back home. They also serve their community. The Methodist bulletin had a whole list of things their congregation was doing."

Sephie reached across the table to pat Corinna's hand. "I'm sorry for what my sister and those biddies did to you. Truly, we do need to swap remedies and stories."

Corinna gave the old woman a weak smile. "You said you needed my help."

"Let's wait on that," Floyd said, noticing Millie coming toward them with a tray. "Here comes something hippity hopping."

Sephie backhanded his arm again, just as James cringed and said, "You did say that."

Corinna just said, "I hope it's not moving."

Chapter 26

Scraping the last crumb of the white cake off her plate, Sephie savored the sweet treat. "I haven't had a good cake in a long time. And this icing!"

Millie picked up her dessert plates to add to those on the tray she carried. "Connie doesn't normally do any baking," she said. "We serve pie because it's pretty easy for the cook to make and people like it. But Connie's niece is getting married and she's making the cake so she's trying a few different flavors."

"If that's the wedding cake," Floyd said, "it's the first one I've had that doesn't taste like soggy cardboard with Crisco icing."

"That's real buttercream," Millie said and headed for the kitchen.

"After the rabbit," Corinna said, "I didn't think I'd have room for a bite of anything more. But this was wonderful." She looked at James. "Thanks for urging me to share yours."

Sephie smiled at the youngsters and how good food could bring people together.

Turning to Floyd, Corinna said, "So, can we talk now about what help you need?"

The old man looked at Sephie, waiting for her to take the lead in explaining their predicament.

"We've had some . . . incidents at my house. Some of it is Agnesia come back to pass judgment on things I do. I can't do anything about that. She hasn't really harmed anyone though she's broken a few things. I figure that might stop once we get her furniture out of the house."

Taking a sip of her iced tea, Sephie stalled for a few minutes. "We had a sending and maybe a possession that I think isn't Agnesia."

"A sending?" Corinna asked. "What kind of sending?"

Sephie hesitated. "A witch ball. Not a little one. But one the size of my fist."

"What did you do about it?"

"Floyd burned it."

Corinna nodded. "You didn't let it touch you, did you?"

Floyd shook his head.

"Do you know who sent it?" she asked.

Sephie shrugged. "I've not intentionally done anything to anybody."

"Jealousy maybe?"

"I don't really mix with the local Grannies and herb women. We do different kinds of healings, and it's been a long time since I even got a call for help. I took all my wares up to North Dakota this summer to my great-niece's shop. They can't get the herbs we have here."

Corinna leaned back against the padded back of the booth. "Are you sure it was sent to you?"

"Well, it sure did move at me whenever I moved. Like it was a dog trying to herd me into a clear space to attack."

"When did this happen?"

Sephie screwed up her face. "Seems like a long time ago."

"Friday," Floyd said, "when your cousin T. Berry and his wife Easter came."

Corinna blinked. "Well, if T. Berry was involved, it could've been aimed at him. A lot of people don't like him."

Looking at Floyd, the old woman said, "But T. Berry was out with you and James."

"It could've come skittering into your house when he was there," James said.

"I didn't see it until well after y'all had left, and it headed

120

toward Easter first."

"But it hunted you," James said.

"Only because Easter was up on a chair like one of those cartoon ladies who'd seen a mouse."

"So, really it could've been sent to anyone at your house."

"And it wasn't sent at Agnesia because she's no longer with us. I mean it's bad enough my sister is carrying on, thumping furniture and breaking things, but somebody sending a witch ball? It doesn't make sense."

Corinna frowned thinking. "Anything else happened?"

Floyd looked at Sephie who didn't seem to want to mention the other bit about a large appliance. "Well, it seems the dishwasher was having a religious experience."

"What?" Both Corinna and James said at once.

"The dishwasher sounded like it was talking," Sephie admitted.

"Speaking in tongues, you said," Floyd added.

"It did sound like that but slower and in a deeper kind of demonic voice. I've heard enough in my time to know what that sounds like. Can we do anything about all this?"

Corinna leaned back against the booth back again. "If you want to keep living in the house, you're going have to do something."

"They're selling," James blurted out. "We're packing, but it's taking time."

"So, you want to get rid of this for the time you're there, then?"

"I don't want to take anything back with me," Sephie said.

"And there are the ethics of selling a house that has these things happening," Floyd said.

Corinna was silent a long moment before straightening to say, "You've got a lot of things going on there. First, I'll need to walk through your house and read it."

Sephie nodded. "I'd do the same with a house blessing. But why can't I read anything?"

"It's hard sometimes to read your own property, too many memories and energies there. I don't know you really. I could pick up what you can't."

"Can you get beyond the fact that she's a Smith?" Floyd asked.

Soberly, the young woman nodded. "She's not like her sister."

"When could you come?" James asked.

Turning to him, she said. "Tomorrow mid-morning. I'll get my intern to cover for me after he comes in." Looking back at Floyd and Sephie, she added, "If that would be convenient?"

"We'll have some food afterwards," Sephie said. "I always need something to ground with when I do that kind of work."

For the first time, Corinna smiled at the old woman. "I'd like to learn about what remedies you put up."

Sephie reached to pat the young woman's hand again. "Thank you for your help."

"I haven't done anything yet. We need to see what you're up against first. It might take the two of us to find a proper remedy. Now, I must be going. Thank you for dinner."

James stood to let her out of the booth. "I'll walk you to your car," he said.

Corinna smiled at him as she walked beside him toward the entrance to the café.

"That boy doesn't have a chance," Sephie said. "I think he may not want to go back home now," Sephie said.

"Oh, he'll go back," Floyd said. "He's got unfinished business there. But that young lady has the means to visit."

Chapter 27

Day 8: Monday, Sephie's home,
Dark Hollow TN, late evening

As the soft, cotton nightdress sprinkled with tiny yellow flowers slipped down over Sephie's tired body, she turned to Floyd, who sat on the bed buttoning the shirt of his blue pajamas. "I have a bone to pick with you," she said.

"Are we picking a turkey carcass?" He stood.

"This isn't something to joke about. You never smothered Yolanda when she was pregnant and dealing with pre-eclampsia. We're old people. We ache and are in pain. Things stop working. Things break. We won't live forever. You gotta stop smothering. Let me live as much as I can while I still can."

Floyd closed the distance between them to put both hands on the sides of her ample waist. "I buried one wife because I didn't pay attention. I didn't care enough."

"You buried your wife because she had cancer, Floyd. You didn't give her cancer. She didn't get it because of neglect." She paused and then blatantly said, "Though you probably broke her heart. But you were there at the end. You made peace, didn't you?"

Floyd turned his head away as some emotion passed over his face. When he finally looked at her again, he said in almost a whisper, "She cursed me every day. Every time I brought her food or gave her medicine or bathed her body. Every single time. She even cursed me for allowing Yolanda to leave and become a flight attendant."

Grasping his upper arms, Sephie said, "And no amount of smothering could change that. And it won't change things now."

Taking a deep breath, the old woman then said, "I took care of myself before you came along. It's been nice, but you've made me rely on you too much." After a pause, she finally admitted, "I love you, Floyd Whiteman. Nothing's going to change that. But allow me space to breathe. Your chivalry has been nice." She smiled. "In the beginning. But if you keep this up, it'll start to look like control. You aren't a controlling man. Don't start now."

Floyd stared at her a long time before pulling her close. "I'm sorry." Squeezing her a little too tightly, he said, "I just don't want to lose you."

Moving away to look at him, she said, "I'm not going anywhere. I'm committed." Then she smiled. "You can still rescue me when I get pigheaded. Sometimes, I don't see where that'll lead."

Without replying, Floyd kissed her intently.

When Sephie got her breath back, she said with a little twinkle in her eye, "Let's make Agnesia slam some furniture around."

Chapter 28

Day 9: Tuesday, Sephie's home,
Dark Hollow TN, midmorning

Floyd lifted down a large 16 x 20 framed color photo of a wedding couple. "You don't have any art on your walls," he observed. "Just photos."

"We've always just hung up photos. The only art you'd see around here would be a picture of Jesus at the Last Supper." Sephie put a piece of cardboard against another framed photo in a box she was filling.

"The one in Agnesia's room that's put on a piece of cedar?"

"She got that in Rock City when she went there on her honeymoon."

Floyd put the big photo on the couch next to other more modest-sized ones already propped against the cushions there. "Is this your daughter and her husband?" he asked.

Sephie walked over to the couch to look at the couple behind the glass. "Yes, that's Debra and Joe. It was taken at a big Baptist church in Knoxville."

"They weren't married here?"

"No, Joe's family were long time members there. That was a big church. It seemed too ornate for a Baptist church, though. It even had a built-in baptismal pool behind the pulpit area. When people got saved, they'd push a button and the curtains would part and the floor would retract like one of those pool covers. It had steps where you could just walk down into the pool. It was huge! You could've put a small choir in there with a couple of deacons while the preacher did the dunking."

She chuckled. "The church was on fifty acres and had a huge cemetery, a ten-acre picnic grounds, and a pavilion for summer meetings and revivals. They even had their own fishing pond. And lordy, their fleet of buses could've transported every child to school in four counties."

Floyd studied the photo. "She was a beautiful bride."

Sephie nodded. "That she was."

"Like her mama."

The old woman waved her hand to dismiss the compliment, but she smiled anyway.

"Shouldn't we pay them a visit before we leave?"

Sephie took in a deep breath. "I suppose."

Turning to her, he stated, "You don't sound excited."

Sephie picked up one of the smaller photos and walked to the box she was filling. "We talked on the phone when I got here. They didn't come for the funeral, but I really didn't expect them to." The old woman put the photo in and wedged another piece of cardboard over the glass.

"Wasn't she worried about you? I'd a thought she would've wanted to be here with you."

"That may've been my fault. I told her I had someone helping."

"Does she know about us?" He handed her another photo. "And that you're selling and moving far away?"

Sephie straightened, frowning. "Debra and Joe have busy lives. They're in Atlanta now." She put the photo in the box and found another piece of cardboard. "I've never been to their home since they moved. It's a long drive. They visit here, but it's been less and less frequent since Agnesia moved in."

"They didn't like your sister?"

"I think it was because they didn't have to worry about me. Agnesia was here."

Floyd frowned as he reached for another frame and uttered a judgmental "Hmmm."

"Hmmm? What's that about?"

126

Putting the photo in her hands, he just said, "Elders should be looked after."

"Young'uns leave home."

"Some. But there's always a sibling or a cousin who'd step in. I don't see anyone here—"

"And who's left taking care of you, old man, now that Yolanda's gone?" Sephie demanded, squaring on him as if she was preparing to throw a punch.

Noticing how Sephie set her jaw, Floyd braced himself for another scolding like the one she given him the night before. But her eyes glistened with something other than fire as if she knew she had stepped over a line. Floyd shut his own mouth against a rebuttal.

The sound of laughter caused them to swivel their heads toward the front door, their expressions set mid-argument.

Corinna, dressed in gray slacks and a vibrant pink blouse, brought a spark of color into the plain living room that was now bare of photos on the walls and bric-a-brac on the tables. Corinna's face was flushed and her eyes sparkled with youthful gaiety. Seeing the old couple staring at her, she immediately sobered, arranging her face into a more dignified professional appearance.

Grinning, James stepped around her, oblivious to the tension in the room. "I found the drug store just fine," he announced in a rush. "Corinna was waiting outside. What do you need me . . . to . . . do?" His voice slowed down, trailing off as he noticed something was amiss. "Or just get out of the way?"

Floyd took a step away from Sephie and the box she was packing. "That's up to Miss Corinna. Every person reads differently." Noticing a cloth bag made from faded flower print upholstery fabric that the young woman clutched from its heavy wooden handled, he asked, "Did you bring smudge?"

"And some other things," she answered crisply.

"Do you do top to bottom or bottom to top?"

Corinna scanned the living room and then up to the ceiling. "There's no cellar, I suppose."

"Not that I found," Floyd said. He turned to Sephie. "Unless I missed a door. A root cellar outside?"

Sephie stirred finally, shaking her head. "Earl thought cellars were old fashioned. He wanted a modern house. We just had a large pantry and a good fridge."

"Attic?" Corinna asked, still staring at the ceiling.

Sephie shook her head again and then added, "No," when the young woman hadn't shifted her gaze.

Finally, looking at the old couple again, she announced, "Top to bottom."

"I don't mean to tell anyone how to practice their art," Sephie began, "but since my sister didn't like you, I don't think you should do this alone."

Corinna thought about that. "It can't be you. You know the house and you have abilities. I don't want anyone projecting into my reading."

"I don't think it should be James," Floyd said. "He's a distraction."

The young woman opened her mouth to protest and then promptly shut it as if to prove she was behaving professionally. "Then it's you," she said.

"Agnesia doesn't like either of us so I'll do it." Floyd said.

Squinting at him, Corinna studied him. "You've been off the Red Road most of your life."

Floyd raised an eyebrow and then looked down embarrassed. After a brief silence, he looked frankly at her. "I had a wild youth that lasted too many years."

"You just started walking the path again. How long have you been sober?"

He took a startled breath and then smiled. "That never was the issue. It was a symptom of chasing a rodeo high."

"What changed?"

"I got old and finally saw that life was a big enough high."

Corinna swung her attention on Sephie. "And you have no clue what you're getting yourself into." She paused. "This isn't home anymore." Then sensing James at her elbow as if he were intruding, she turned to him. "Your feet have stumbled but only because you didn't know where the road was leading you. Go where the loon calls." Corinna blinked and took a couple of shaky steps to a nearby armchair. She sat down heavily.

"James, get her a glass of lemonade from the fridge," Sephie ordered and carefully approached the young woman. "You opened quickly."

Instantly, James returned, offering a frosty glass under Corinna's nose. She took it and drank a long draught of the sweet liquid. "This house." She took another sip and then narrowed her eyes at the old woman. "You must automatically barrier." She looked at the two men who were also hovering over her. To James, she said, "You can't sense." Then turning to Floyd and finally to Sephie. "You both barrier out of habit."

"Barrier?" Sephie asked. "You mean shield?" She shrugged. "I've had to hide what I do for most of my life, especially the last ten years. And recently we both have had to shield heavily because we'd been dealing with something up North."

"You and your family have imbued this house with energy since it was built. It's just charged—" Then she seemed distracted, looking up again. "But there's something." She returned to Sephie's face. "You said the witch ball was in the kitchen."

Sephie stepped back and the men made space so that the old woman could point in the direction of the kitchen toward the back of the house.

"Show me," Corinna demanded as she stood. Looking up at Floyd, she added, "Stay close."

The old man merely nodded.

Chapter 29

Day 9: Tuesday, Sephie's home,
Dark Hollow TN, late morning

James hesitated before he followed the rest into the kitchen. Things didn't feel right. He'd seen the old pair bicker before, but there was always a large scoop of caring behind it. From Sephie's posture and how she clenched her jaw indicated there was heavy ammunition behind whatever they were arguing about. He'd gotten used to the solidity between them; something he never really saw with his grandparents or even really his parents. The fights between his kin would often degenerate into flinging china or fists. Sephie was good for the old man, but he didn't think she knew she was the glue that held his spirit together.

His own spirit had begun to take wings as he'd talked and laughed with Corinna in Floyd's truck. Those wings, however, had begun to take deep strokes just to stay aloft when she started reading everybody. James had always heard stories about the old men who carried medicine bundles who could tell if you told a lie. But he felt they were just stories to tell kids to own up to something they did. Still, Corinna had been right about needing to go home.

Walking into the kitchen now where he'd had many home-cooked meals, he wondered if Corinna had just said what she had because she'd just been very observant. She would have to be in order to do the traditional medicine she did that complemented her modern career.

"You said the witch ball came in here," Corinna stated.

"Yes," Sephie said. "I was over here by the stove and my

cousin Easter was at the table wrapping plates and putting them in boxes."

Corinna paced around the table. "Where'd you get the boxes?"

"James and I got them from the grocery store," Floyd said.

"Were they open boxes, no tops?"

"Some were," Sephie said. "There were a number of them that still had the flaps so you could reseal them."

"Had you looked in them before you started packing?"

"They all seemed empty. I've been using a bunch to pack books." She pointed to a vacant corner near the laundry room door where three boxes stood. "I put the dishes I want to keep there. The other boxes of dishes were taken to the thrift store."

Corinna looked closely at Sephie's face. "Can you be sure that the witch ball wasn't in one of the boxes?"

"Well, no. But they did seem to be empty. I only had newspapers in the boxes. I'd a thought Easter would have told me if she found something in one of them."

Again, the young woman walked around the table. "Where was Easter standing?"

Sephie pointed to the side of the table nearest her. "About there beside the first chair. An empty box was on it."

"So, what happened?"

"I had my back turned. Easter screamed and pointed at the thing. I saw—"

"Where was it?"

"On the other side of the table. Though Easter was over here near me, every time she moved it twitched toward her."

"Then what happened?"

"She climbed onto another chair and the thing headed for me, countering every move I made as if to block any escape. I got it into the pantry and shut the door."

"Can you describe it?"

"About yay-big," Sephie said cupping her hands until they made a ball about the size of a baseball or tennis ball. It was made of gray hair with things — bits of leaves and stuff — stuck in it like it'd rolled over the ground."

"Gray hair," Corinna repeated eyeing Sephie's head.

Raising an eyebrow and stiffening, the old woman snapped, "Not mine. A different color, paler. Mine's steel gray. This wasn't and it seemed softer, thinner."

Corinna just nodded. "I'll read down here first. Then upstairs. Once that's done, I'll smudge and chant top to bottom." She looked up at Floyd. "You know a song?"

He nodded. "Protection."

"I have a rattle." Turning to Sephie, she asked, "What would you do to bless a house?"

"The same. Except I'd also bless with salt water and place obsidian around. I don't have any now, but there's plenty of salt. Then I'd invoke the blessings of hearth and home with spices. Two passes in total."

Nodding, Corinna said, "Follow us when we smudge." She turned to James. "Help her." Giving each person in the room a long look, she added, "Normally, I'd consult after the read, but I'm already picking up something. We need to act and not talk. I think your sister pissed off someone very powerful, and she's not done. We need to seal this house."

For the first time, James shuddered as if someone had walked over his grave.

Chapter 30

Day 9: Tuesday, Sephie's home,
Dark Hollow TN, noonish

Corinna did a cursory reading of the rest of the first floor, ending with Sephie's sitting room. As she left to go upstairs, she raised an eyebrow at Sephie, who stood outside that room, waiting to enter to procure her blessing supplies. "Keep this door closed," the young woman said. "It's clear."

Sephie entered with James at her heels as if he didn't want to be left alone in the house. "Close the door," she ordered James as she pulled down a large tin box from an empty bookshelf. She placed it on a side table beside an armchair and a floor lamp, the only furnishings in the room besides the bookshelves, whose contents had been packed away in boxes that were stacked along one of them

Rummaging through the box, she pulled out small plastic containers of whole cloves, crushed cinnamon sticks, basil, rosemary, bay leaves, lavender, and rose hips. From the tin, she also pulled out a ceramic bowl that bore a dark blue glaze emblazoned with pale blue spots, making it look as if it were made naturally from snowflake obsidian. She also found a stemless brandy snifter and a plastic container of salt inside the box.

Handing the ceramic bowl to James, she said, "Go fill that half way with water from the kitchen tap."

By the time he returned, she had unscrewed the lids of all of the small containers and was opening the container of salt. Looking at the boy's face, she explained, "This is Zuni salt. My great-niece found a man online who supplies her with it. It comes from New Mexico from a place where the salt comes up out of the ground and solidifies every year. Native people gather it and use it for table salt. But there are some who say it is sacred. I brought some back with me. I'll use it sparingly."

James seemed to relax as she added salt to the water in the bowl he held.

Stirring the water with her hand, she said, "Behold creature of art. Water and earth. Cleansing and creating, mirroring the great salt sea from whence we came and to which we will return. Purify the space we bless and those who bless it."

She sprinkled a bit over James, who stood with his head bowed, and then finally herself. "So let it be." As Sephie put herbs and spices into the brandy snifter, she wished she had some Florida water that Mandy and Laura's friend Patricia used. She would just mix everything with a bit of the salt water. She told James the properties of each herb and spice. When she added cinnamon and cloves, she said, "For the blessings of hearth and home. For sweetness that satisfies all hunger." When she added basil and rosemary, she said, "For prosperity and lack of want." She added the last three ingredients and said, "For love and harmony within."

A loud thud from upstairs jolted them from their ministrations. Sephie looked up. "Guess Agnesia doesn't like Corinna up there."

Picking up the brandy snifter in one hand, she dipped her free hand into the salt water and sprinkled it over the contents she held, then she offered it to James. She took his heavy bowl from him and motioned toward the door. "We might as well wait in the living room. We have to open the front door when they start to smudge."

"Why?" James said closing the door behind them when they left the room.

"Whatever energies they banish have to go somewhere. So, out the door." Easing herself down onto the edge of an armchair, Sephie added, "When they come down the stairs, we'll go up."

The sound of a rattle and Floyd's high chant drifted down to them, causing Sephie to look up at the ceiling. There was another thud, then a crash, followed by a steady rapping as if the legs of a chair or bed were being repeatedly struck against the linoleum. A whine like that of a summer storm began, rising in volume and strength until it was a roar. Floyd's chant paused a moment after a human grunt and the sound of another thud, less bulky as the ones before as if someone had fallen.

Sephie shot to her feet.

Floyd's chant resumed and the rattle was almost masked by the sound of the wind. An eerie keening joined the wind, wavering in an out in loudness as if someone had tried to tune into a radio station during a storm. Then the whole house shook causing Sephie to run to the front door, open it, and look at the clear blue sky outside. It was then that she felt the initial touch of the wind from upstairs. She stepped away to yell at James, "Go bring one of those boxes from the kitchen to brace the door open."

He put the brandy snifter on a nearby end table and hurried to the kitchen.

The front door was waffling as if it would slam shut at any moment. Sephie grabbed it with her free hand and pushed her ample backside against it to hold it open. James rushed in and placed the box on the floor as Sephie moved away.

"Get the glass of herbs!" Sephie yelled as the roar and rush of wind reached them. He had just picked it up when the full force of the gale swirled around them. There was nothing to show it was there. No fog. No dark cloud. No electrical force. Just the power of the wind and the noise — unintelligible voices, shrieks, threats that couldn't quite be made out except for a stray word here and there. "Hate y—" "curse up—" "die" "abomination." But worse than all that was the sheer evil in the wind. It soured Sephie's stomach, making her want to retch. She looked at James to see how he was and he just looked scared to death.

Floyd's chanting seemed louder now, causing Sephie to turn toward the stairs. He and Corinna were headed toward the kitchen.

"Upstairs," Sephie ordered.

They trudged through the wind that was swirling newspapers and even lifting rectangles of cardboard Sephie had piled beside a box to protect family photos. Reaching the stairs, they started up, Sephie dragging herself up by the stair rail. James followed close behind her. The wind began to abate as they reached the landing and started down the hall to the farthest bedroom, the one James was using. Entering it, Sephie did a quick read. It was totally naked, devoid of any energy whatsoever. The old woman frowned. That wasn't good. Anything could rush into that void. Immediately, she started sprinkling salt water in the corners of the room.

"Sprinkle behind me. Think of Christmas, birthdays, the best gig you ever played with an audience that loved your music. Great food. Anything happy that you can think of."

So, they proceeded as the wind died down and the noises from downstairs quieted. Room by room, bathroom, closets, even bureau drawers. On and on, ending up finally downstairs through all of the rooms until they were in Sephie's sitting room, which only needed a brief blessing. After pouring the salt water down the kitchen sink and casting the last of the herbed water out the front door, Sephie washed her ritual ware and put them back into the tin box.

At Sephie's bidding, James brought in the boxes from the kitchen and put them with the boxes of books. Since, Corinna had indicated that her sitting room was protected, Sephie felt that all of the items they'd transport would be stored in that room or outside on the porch. Finally, she sat her weary body down on a chaise lounge on front porch and drifted off to sleep.

Chapter 31

Day 9: Tuesday, Connie's,
East Hollow Gap, KY, midafternoon

The pile of spaghetti smothered in marinara sauce, extra cheese, and several fat meatballs filled a void that James hadn't realized was there. The heavy meal not only sated James' hunger from today's activities but settled him squarely in the present more than he thought a plate of food could. What he had witnessed was not just disturbing, but it shattered a few of his twenty-first century constructs. When Corinna had discussed the plan to read, cleanse, and bless Sephie's house, it all seemed harmless. The reading sounded like it could be just pure intuition mixed with observations, even though they had uncannily hit home to everyone she had read. The smudging was no different from what he'd seen at ceremonies all his life. And, the salt water sprinkling was similar to having a priest come bless a new house with holy water. Sephie's final blessing with herbs should have been just an aesthetic touch. It was what all that had stirred up that troubled him. Scanning the faces around the table around him, who were also wolfing down copious amounts of pasta, made him wonder if their activities had been a serious mistake that no one wanted to talk about.

About half way through his plate, he leaned back from the table and drank down a generous amount of a Summerfest lager. Studying everyone, he finally voiced what no one had been inspired to say. "Anyone ever experience what happened today before?"

Beside him, Corinna stopped chewing the forkful of spaghetti she had deftly maneuvered into her mouth that was bent over her plate. She turned her head to stare at him.

Floyd just put up his hands in front of him and then picked up his iced tea, drinking deeply.

Sephie pushed her plate away from her and closed her eyes as she eased back against the hard booth. She reached into her purse, rummaged around inside, and pulled out a bottle of ibuprofen. Shaking three out into her hand, she picked up her own glass of tea and finally downed the pain relievers. Once that was done, she finally looked at James and just shook her head.

Craning his head toward Corinna, he raised an eyebrow. She swallowed and then drank half of the generous portion of house red in her glass.

Turning back to Sephie and Floyd, James said, "You do realize that we have to sleep there tonight. Or are we going to take turns sleeping in the truck?"

Floyd tilted his head toward Corinna.

When she didn't reply, James simply stated, "I've got first dibs on the truck."

Chapter 32

Day 9: Tuesday, Sephie's home,
Dark Hollow TN, evening

"We have to tell the boy something," Floyd said taking off his plaid shirt to get ready for bed.

"I don't know what to tell him," Sephie admitted, brushing her hair vigorously as if she could rid it of today's events. "I don't know myself."

"Corinna needs to talk to us about what she sensed," he said.

"I know, but she's not saying a word. The look on her face was enough to know it was bad. Did you pick up anything?"

"I don't have those gifts, Sephie, you know that. All I felt was evil."

"But you sense stuff about people. Is Corinna on the level? Could something have hijacked in on her when she started to work?"

"Again, I'm not the one to ask." Buttoning up his pajama top, he walked to Sephie. "We need to talk to her away from here."

"We can't go eating out any more. It's costing a fortune. Connie's food is good, but we can both cook her something fit to eat. But we need to talk to her." She asked again. "Are you sure you didn't pick up something?

"All I know is that we stirred up something."

"And then she cleaned everything out. It was down to absolutely nothing in the house and that's not right. Every house has energy from living, from even the building of it. This was totally stripped."

Touching her shoulders, he encouraged, "But you and James put good things back. It isn't so empty now."

"I don't know. Agnesia's furniture is still here. She could've left a remnant."

"I'll call a consignment shop from the next town in the morning and have them come take some of the furniture. We can leave this bed and James' and the kitchen table and chairs."

Sephie nodded. "That will be a good start. I'll work on everything up here. The closets and bathroom. Pack up all the bedding and clothes, I guess."

"And James and I will go down to that cabin of yours and dismantle that propane fridge. I can use it in my fish house this winter, if it's alright with you."

"How're you going to transport that thing up the mountain?"

"Somehow you got it down there."

"I had B.D. and a bunch of his college buddies to help. They manhandled it down there with all of the building supplies."

"Too bad I can't dismantle that cabin."

"It'd take you two weeks to do that. It's not worth you busting your back or worse to try to make a new fish house out of that."

He chuckled, putting his arms around her. "Guess not."

"And James can't spend the rest of his time here sleeping in the truck. Even the chaise lounge on the porch would be better."

"Well, you had a nice nap in it today."

"I think it was sheer exhaustion."

"James'll be alright. He may have been born to the rez, but he's really a city boy at heart. He didn't go fishing and hunting with his granddad like I did, sleeping in the wild. He and his cousins had fancy dome tents and all of the comforts of home except for TV. I think the truck is familiar. I'm sure he spent many a night sleeping in his car or the band van when he was touring."

She nodded. "I suppose." She sighed. "I just never wanted to bring the boy into our troubles. . . . Or my troubles. I really didn't want it to even affect you."

He smiled. "We're in this together." After a little pause, he said, "Today, you asked who's taking care of me?" There were amused wrinkles around his eyes. "You are. And I'm taking care of you." Then he kissed her a good long time. When he raised his head, he also raised an eyebrow to the silence in the house. "Quiet."

"Shhh," Sephie said. "Don't jinx it."

Chapter 33

Floyd hoisted the box of canning jars out of the truck bed and stepped toward the porch were Sephie's cousin Lige waited. "Sephie thought you'd have better use of these than she will."

"She not planning on doing any canning up north?"

He shook his head and placed the box on the painted floor of the porch.

"Sit a spell," Lige offered. "Time for a sip."

As Floyd sat once more in the porch swing, he shook his head.

"You a teetotler like Agnesia or did you like it too much?"

"Not really," Floyd admitted. "It's not something I enjoy if I ever did."

The fat man nodded. "You ever taste my brew?"

"I had a sip of the butterscotch."

Lige laughed. "It tastes like candy, but it sneaks up on you." He paused. "I have some blackberry I just drew off. Want a thimbleful?"

Floyd smiled, sensing that there was some sort of bonding test he offered and gave his head a tilt in acceptance.

In no time at all, Lige came out with a jigger for Floyd and a tumbler half full of the clear liquid for himself. When he had settled into his plastic-webbed rocker, he raised his glass in salute to his visitor.

Floyd chugged down the small offering, thinking it would be as smooth as the fat man's butterscotch. Instead, it burned his esophagus all the way down to hit his stomach hard. His mouth, however, was left with distinct taste of cooked blackberries. "Jesus, Mary, and Joseph!" he spat out, catching his breath.

Lige just laughed. "Should've warned you." He took another drink from his own glass. "Somebody told me that they set some afire and poured it over ice cream. Said it tasted like blackberry ice cream."

"I can see that," Floyd said, leaning back. "It's got enough alcohol in it."

"Sephie's husband Earl couldn't handle the stuff. But that was pretty much how he was with most things we did when we was young."

"How do you mean?"

"He grew up with us because one of his brothers married Sephie's other sister, Bess."

"Another sister?"

Lige nodded. "There were five in the family, three girls and two boys. The boys died young — war. Bess passed — oh gosh — thirty years ago. She and Earl's oldest brother were evangelists, and they went off on some missionary work in India or Borneo, some godforsaken place or other. She'd been the oldest. Earl had four brothers and no sisters. All older and they were out of the house before Earl and Sephie got hitched."

"Who's Mandy's grandfather?"

"Earl's brother George. He was a great fiddle player if I remember. Been gone a long time. Died in the mines before his baby boy was born." Taking another sip from his glass, he considered and amended. "Come to think of it, that's not right. Mandy's mom married Earl's son and then divorced him. She remarried a Branscombe who was a widower who had a baby girl, Mandy."

"So, they're only related by marriage."

"Didn't Sephie tell you all this?"

"We talked some about family. But we both have lots of

146

kin. It can be hard to keep up." He paused. "You were telling me about Earl."

"Oh yeah." Lige took another swig from his glass. "Earl grew up with all of us. But he was really more of a city boy. I mean the boy could shoot. Lordy, we hunted with .22 longs, and he could shoot a squirrel out of a tree before we could even find the varmint up there. Seems his daddy had the same eagle eye, making him and his brothers in demand by the US Army during World War II. They liked all those Tennessee and Kentucky boys because they were such good shots. Lawd, today's military is run by kids who fly drones like they're in a computer game!"

"Earl do a lot of hunting?"

"More when he was young. We all did to feed our families. When Earl got that good job of his, he stopped going out with us." Lige laughed again, shaking his head. "He was always tryin' to think he was better than us — though never puttin' us down, mind you. But one fall night, we'd been huntin' all day and not bagged very much. We'd all decided to sleep in the woods that night and get up early and try again. We'd built a small campfire, but it wudn't big enough to warm us on that chilly night as we laid out in our coats on the ground. Well, we all got up in the mornin', and Earl was gone. We thought he'd gone out to take his mornin' constitutional in the bushes. We called out to him and looked around but couldn't find him. As we were searchin', we found his trail to a farmstead. In the back, closest to the woods, there was a corn crib, full of that year's dried corn. As we neared, we could hear this loud snorin'.

"Sure enough, Earl had found hisself a nice cushy bed for the night. I looked at my brothers, and we both seemed of the same mind. I went over to the corncrib, pulled out a book of matches and lit those dry husks. Soon the shucks took fire and started to smoke. Pretty soon Earl woke up, jumped up yellin', and climbed out of that corn crib so fast!" He laughed.

147

Floyd didn't quite see the humor in it. "What if something would've happened?"

"Oh, we would've fetched him out of there. But he was laughin' about it when he saw us all." After taking a sip from his glass, he commented, "That's one thing you could say about Earl. He sure could take a joke." Looking straight at Floyd, he added, "He always knew he wudn't one of us exactly. But he was all right." He paused. "You hunt?"

Knowing there was more in that innocent question, Floyd just smiled. "I have. But not for a while."

"Whatcha hunt?"

"Small game sometimes." He watched Lige nod. Then he added, "Turkey, deer, pronghorn. Missed a moose by inches once."

"What kind of fire power?"

"Ought .38 Winchester."

Lige raised an eyebrow before raising his glass to his lips again.

"My granddad's gun," Floyd added like swathing icing over a cake. He hadn't intended to brag, but since he was to become part of this family, he didn't want Sephie to be ashamed of him.

"You teach your son?"

Floyd shook his head. "Only had one daughter but her husband was a decent hunter. And my granddaughter, as modern and independent as she is, never wanted to learn to shoot."

Lige nodded. "Women usually don't want to learn."

"I plan on teaching Sephie how to use a handgun. We'll be living out in the country. There are bobcats and mountain lions around and badgers. They can get mean."

Lige chuckled. "I'd like to see that. What do you carry?"

"An old Colt, but it's too heavy for her. I'll have to get her a lighter one."

"Sephie, markswoman." He chuckled again.

"What can you tell me about her daughter and her husband?

They're in Atlanta, aren't they?"

The fat man nodded. "Debra always was uppity. She married rich and that's how she likes it. I don't think how she turned out had much to do with Sephie. It's backwards from what Sephie values."

"Did Earl value money?"

He shrugged. "He liked making money. Was a bit too tight-fisted with it, if you ask me. He could've made Sephie's life a bit easier. Do you know she didn't get a washer and dryer until he'd passed and Agnesia moved in. Agnesia demanded. And she wanted a dishwasher. So, Sephie bought them from what was left of the insurance money. The house was already paid for by the time Earl passed so that was good. And Earl had signed over his retirement to Sephie so she could maintain the house. Sephie never worked in her life. Worked outside the house. She did a lot of canning and sewing, and it took time raising Debra. She didn't marry until she was almost 30."

Nodding, Floyd eased himself off the porch swing. "Thanks for the taste, Lige. I must be getting back." He offered his hand for Lige to shake, which he did.

As Floyd stepped off the porch, Lige called back, "Did Pollard's girl help y'all out?"

Offering a small smile, Floyd reminded himself he still had to pick up Corinna for dinner. "Yes. Thanks. We appreciate your help."

Chapter 34

Day 10: Wednesday, Sephie's home,
Dark Hollow TN, early evening

The fried catfish that Floyd fixed was a surprise to Sephie, who wondered if he was a quick study from the description of the meal they had at Connie's or he always cooked it that way. It was filleted very thin, breaded in both flour and cornmeal, and quickly fried in hot oil. Sephie's potato salad and a plate of her precious farm tomatoes rounded out the meal, which was indeed served in the kitchen.

Floyd interrupted the quiet of the meal. "Corinna, we really need to know exactly what happened here yesterday."

"What do you mean?" she asked. "You were all here."

"I, for one, don't know what happened," James said. "I've never seen anything like that before. Hell, I've never heard of anything like that. The freakiest thing I've ever heard about was that tall tale about Robert Johnson selling his soul to the Devil so he could be a good bluesman."

Corinna stared at him, not in disbelief but with a look of something else. "That sure has a lot of deep layers," she said. Swinging to look back at Floyd, she leaned back and said, "What do you want to know?"

"Do you normally clean a house so thoroughly?" Sephie demanded before Floyd could answer.

"It was necessary."

"Because?" the old woman prompted.

Corinna looked down briefly before taking a deep breath and asking, "Who all lived in this house before you?"

"No one. We built this on vacant land."

"Who's lived here?"

"Just my husband and me and our daughter. Agnesia came after Earl died."

The young woman frowned. "You piss anyone off?"

"Me?"

"You don't seem ill-intentioned. But someone did."

Floyd stared up at the ceiling, as if he knew full well who that person was.

"Oh," Sephie mumbled, making the same realization she suspected Floyd did.

James searched each face around the table, his gaze finally resting on Sephie. "Your sister?"

"Unless she's also been doing some dark mojo on the side," Corinna speculated.

"That'd be the day," Sephie grunted. "No, she was very into God."

"Sometimes that can be just as dark when it's filled with hate and constant disapproval." She shook her head. "But this was . . . different."

Sephie tilted her head, not knowing what to think. She eased herself up and went to the coffeemaker. She poured two cups of coffee and set them in front of Floyd and then Corinna. She raised an eyebrow at James, who nodded. "So how was this different?" Sephie asked Corinna and went to pour two more cups when she almost bumped into Floyd, who had also gotten up. "Whoa there, old man. Honk next time."

Floyd chuckled as he picked up a berry cobbler and four small plates and took them to the table.

As Sephie put the coffee in front of James, he grinned at her. She wondered what that was about as she sat down beside him. "You were saying about different."

"I've seen some pretty negative stuff around here. But this—" She shook her head. "This was dark."

"How can you just step in and do what you did without knowing exactly what you're dealing with?" James challenged.

She frowned at him and then studied her coffee before taking a sip. "I had to do something. I couldn't just walk away. I had to get rid of it." She looked up at the ceiling. "I think I did. But. . . ."

"But?" Sephie and James said at the same time.

"This was a working I don't know, gnarled and tangled, and — well foreign."

"Foreign?" It was Floyd's turn to echo one of her words. "Not local mountain Grannies or native folk?"

She shook her head. "Something else." She leaned over the table. "That's why I can't be sure it's over."

"You mean it'll come back?" James squeaked out.

Glancing briefly at the young man, Corinna returned to study Sephie's face. She finally said, "It was tied into the very wood of your sister's furniture. You need to get rid of that."

"The consignment store is coming out tomorrow," Floyd announced.

"Show them where the room is and what goes," she said to Floyd. "Then just step outside as if you're a crotchety granddad who wanted to make sure everything was going into the truck securely. Let them dismantle the bed and carry everything out themselves. Then go in and smudge again with the windows open. I think you'll be alright doing that."

"But what makes you think it's not over?" Sephie demanded.

"I— Find out if there's something under her bed."

"You mean a root?" Sephie asked.

Corinna questioned the old woman's face.

"A conjure tool. B.D. told me about them." Resting back heavily into her chair, Sephie said, "We gotta call him and get him to get Papa Mamoud to help us." She explained to Corinna. "He's a griot and conjure doctor."

"Some native people from Central America put things under the bed, too."

"A raw egg. Yes, I know. But that's to draw the bad stuff into it." Turning to James, she asked, "Didn't you say you'd heard talk about a conjure doctor at Connie's?"

"Shoot! I never did call about that," James said.

"Best you should do that, and I'll call B.D.," Sephie said, then reached across the table to touch Corinna's hand. "Tell us everything you felt. Describe it in detail. I'll need that for B.D."

"Why don't you just call him and have her tell him over the phone?" Floyd suggested.

Sephie grunted. "You are good for something, old man, besides being a pretty face."

Floyd laughed and gave her shoulders a squeeze.

Chapter 35

Day 10: Wednesday, The North Star,
Riverbend ND, evening

The tall lanky Black man paraded into the North Star from the back room. He made a twirl, showing off his suit. "What do you think?"

Mandy whistled from behind the counter and Laura came out to walk around the young man, smoothing out his shoulders in the back of the jacket and even lifted up the tail to look at the fit of the suit's trousers.

"Watch it there, girl. Remember you're a married woman," Mandy teased, causing Laura to give her a very motherly scowl.

Facing the front of the suit, she adjusted the lapels. "B.D. You lucked out. How in the world St. Gertrude's got an Armani suit for their garage sale is beyond me!"

"Armani?" he asked innocently.

She backhanded his chest. "You went right for the label, didn't you?"

"Well, I did notice that."

"The length is right, isn't' it?" Mandy asked.

Laura looked down at B.D.'s shoes. "Yes." She glanced up at him. "What'd it cost?"

"Thirty dollars."

"For a $3000 suit?" Mandy exclaimed.

"It probably is an outdated style."

"Armani is timeless." Stepping back to take in his whole silhouette, Laura brought down her own pronouncement. "You'll shine in all those churches you sing at."

"It's the wedding I'm singing at this weekend I was worried about," B.D. said. "I didn't want to look shabby."

"Trust me," Laura said, giving his shoulder one final flick with her hand. "You'll make any groom here look shabby in his rented tux."

A cellphone rang from the back room.

"Let me get that," B.D. said, heading to the bathroom in the back where he'd left his street clothes. When he picked up the phone he'd left on the edge of the sink, he checked caller ID. Swiping it to accept the call, he said, "Miss Sephie, how's it going?"

"Well. . . ." the old woman began. "I've got a situation here. You got time to talk for a bit?"

"Sure, I need to get out of this suit I bought first. Let me put you on speaker."

"You're at a clothing store?"

"No, I'm at the North Star. I got an Armani suit at St. Gertrude's garage sale. It fits like it was made for me."

"Can't wait to see you in it."

As B.D. shed clothes, he asked, "So, what's up?"

"I think we have a situation here that needs your help or at least Papa Mamoud's."

He paused as he unzipped his new trousers. "That is serious. Tell me about it."

"We found a local girl here to help with a house clearing. She and Floyd did the nasty stuff. She's native, too, and, well, she cleared it to the bone."

Putting on his jeans, he frowned. "That nasty?"

"It must've been. I've never seen that done before. But she says it was ingrained deep into the house. Says it probably came from someone my sister pissed off. It was foreign to her so I figured it might be some conjurer. Did you know of anyone back here who practiced?"

Now dressed, B.D. took his phone into the store. "Well, I'd heard a tale or two, but I never ran into anyone who did.

'Course there're always the cookbook types."

"Say what?"

"You know, what Laura says are the wannabe New Agers. They get a book and think they can just jump right in without protocols and training in place."

"Could be."

"What did you experience?"

"Not a lot. Agnesia was thumping furniture around a lot and breaking things. She didn't like Floyd. But there were a couple of weird things. My dishwasher seemed to be possessed and was speaking in tongues."

Mandy let out a laugh that made Laura glower at her.

"Is that Mandy?" Sephie asked.

"Yes, she's here with Laura. The store's empty so you can talk."

"Good. Then we won't have to repeat ourselves."

"We?" B.D. asked.

"The girl who helped. Corinna."

"Anything else happen besides the dishwasher?" Laura asked.

"We had a visitation by a witch ball."

"What!" Laura almost screeched.

"Somebody sent it. And I think it was directed at me or seemed to be. Those things can corner you like a hound dog."

"Did it touch you?" Laura asked.

"No. I lured it into the pantry and then Floyd and I captured it and burned it outside."

"How big?" Laura demanded.

"Size of a baseball. Made of light gray hair and stuck with leaves and stuff as if it'd rolled in from a distance."

"It probably did," Laura speculated. "Those things can travel for miles if the hate's powerful enough. When did this happen?"

"Oh lord, I don't remember. It was a few days after the funeral."

"So, well after your sister had passed. Was there mention about her in the newspaper?"

"Sure, not much other kind of news to report. Nothing happens here. Maybe a joy ride that ended in a crash or somebody arrested for hitting his wife . . . again. Church sales and new baby pictures. Or a rant about the government."

"Can this girl — Corinna. Can she tell us what she picked up?" B.D. asked.

"That's why I'm calling. I'll put her on the phone, and she'll tell you."

Chapter 36

Day 10: Wednesday, Sephie's home,
Dark Hollow TN, evening

The clear liquid filled the vintage jelly glass nearly up to Wylie Coyote's puffed-up chest. Like him, Sephie wondered when the next anvil would fall.

"That's not a good idea," Floyd said, coming into the kitchen where Sephie was pouring Lige's butterscotch brew from a Mason jar.

Sephie frown deepened. "You're always telling me to have a little."

Picking up the glass, Floyd said, "A little Jameson is good for your bones. But not this stuff." He poured the entire contents of the glass back into the jar. "This stuff is something you don't want to come back up later. Now, a nice relaxing glass of wine would do you a world of good."

"Ain't got any," Sephie said.

"Who says?" Floyd said, putting the Mason jar into the fridge and pulling out a bottle hidden way in the back behind a row of condiments.

"Where'd that come from?"

"James brought it for Miss Corinna when she came to read the house," he said, applying a corkscrew to the bottle of Pinot Grigio. "The boy had forgotten it in the truck with all the confusion and asked me to put it in the fridge while you were napping." Finding a tumbler, he filled it half full and handed it to Sephie. "You go relax on the porch and enjoy the night air."

Sephie reluctantly made her way to the porch and stretched out. She noticed that the front drive was empty still. James

159

hadn't returned from taking Corinna home. The past few days felt as if someone had taken the familiarity of the life she had once known and shook it as if to get wind under a blanket to replace it on a bed. Some things had shifted and others had been lost forever.

She sipped her wine while Floyd moved the glass table between them to the far side of another chaise that he shoved close against Sephie's. He stretched out, put his arm around her, and pulled her close.

"It's good we're leaving this place," the old woman said finally. "I want to stay a day or two in Riverbend when we get up North?"

"You miss Mandy and Laura."

"And B.D. Though it's so different up there."

"It has its own woo-woo though."

Sephie exhaled wearily. "Yes, but—"

"But it's not here," Floyd finished for her. "It's hard to deal with a hard truth about someone of your own blood that could stir up such evil."

"I—" she began but took another sip of wine instead. "For ten years she was in this house. Ten years! And I just thought she just didn't approve of me. I had no idea she'd set up her own little Gestapo. I mean I thought it was kind of absurd how she'd call the preacher on me."

"For what?"

She shrugged. "Living. I just think she liked his attention. But to find out someone or multiple someones were upset enough with her to send things at me. I haven't done anything. Shoot, I'm probably more like them in their practices."

"But Corinna was stumped. This wasn't a local Granny or a conjure doctor."

Twisting her head off of Floyd's shoulder to try to look at him, Sephie said, "We never called them that. I thought it was some bayou thing that B.D. knew about. But even he thought this was different."

"Could it be a group?"

"Sure, it's a group," Sephie fussed. "Corinna said there were multiple sendings."

"But I mean working together."

"You mean like a coven or something."

"Or just people come together to launch an attack."

"Agnesia is dead and buried. Why send stuff here?"

"Corinna said some of what she picked up had been here a long time, maybe from the beginning."

"I don't believe that."

Floyd didn't respond.

"You believe that, don't you?" she pressed.

The old man took a long breath. "Well, it could just be your name. Maybe some people didn't like Lige making whiskey. Maybe others didn't like your sister or your cousin T. Berry. Maybe one of the church ladies didn't like you making remedies. Maybe somebody was jealous." He scratched his head. "Do you think we brought something back here from up North?"

"You mean like from that jealous store owner in Riverbend?" Sephie thought about that. "Lordy," was all she said before downing the last of her wine.

Floyd took her glass and put it on the little table beside him.

When he turned back to her, she speculated, "But that woman had no power."

"That woman was able to drain your energy just by you walking by her store. Don't underestimate jealousy. And remember when Corinna tried to explain everything to B.D., she said more than one person and some of it was directed at you."

"Well, let's just wait and see what Papa Mamoud says. But I'll tell you one thing. I'd face those bitter winters with you gladly than another summer day here."

Floyd pulled her close. "We'll be home soon, Sephie." He shifted into a more comfortable position. "Let's just sleep out here tonight. We can listen to the katydids better out here."

"You do like sleeping in the wild, don't you?"

"It reminds me of my youth."

"Well, don't think about reclaiming that youthful energy out here. James is still sleeping in the truck and he's got big ears and eyes."

Floyd chuckled and kissed the top of her head.

Chapter 37

Day 11: Thursday, Sephie's home,
Dark Hollow TN, early morning

The dew lay heavy on the quilt as Sephie opened her eyes to a foggy morning as she lay on her left side. She was warm under the covers but realized that her backside wasn't supplemented by Floyd's additional heat. The old woman ventured a hand behind her to find that the quilt had been carefully tucked around her, but her intended was absent. Shifting onto her back, she noticed Floyd's old truck had finally made it back to the driveway. She couldn't tell from where she lay whether James was asleep inside. Hearing the creak of the front door, the old woman turned to find Floyd coming out with two cups of coffee.

"That for me?" she asked, sitting up.

"One of them."

Taking the warm cup into her hands, she muttered, "There are reasons to keep you."

He chuckled and sat down carefully at the foot of her chaise. Though they were sturdy deck chairs with thick cushions, his added weight could topple both of them.

"What time is it?" Sephie asked.

"You got an appointment?"

She shrugged. "It's early. But it's hard to tell with the fog," she said. "When did James get in?"

"Late. He brought us the quilt."

"Had a lot to talk over with Corinna I'm sure."

"Uh-huh," he muttered before drinking his coffee.

"You think, they're—"

"It's none of our business."

"'Suppose," she admitted, taking refuge in her own cup.

"The consignment company comes early so it's good we're up. You'll have to tell them what you want them to take."

"Corinna said you have to. I'll just tell you before they come."

"James will probably spend most of his day rehearsing." He looked around the porch. "Did you put an electric outlet out here?"

"Whatever for?" she asked. "The house was built in the early 60s. We're lucky to get two outlets in each room."

"Got an extension cord?"

"A couple somewhere. Why?"

"I want to set up James out here to practice. He hasn't touched his guitar since Sunday."

"He's that skittish about the house?"

"He's still sleeping in the truck and seeing us out here last night didn't bolster much confidence."

Sephie sighed. "That poor boy, getting roped into something he shouldn't have been involved with." She sipped her coffee. "Did you get what you needed from the cabin in the holler?"

He nodded and motioned toward a nebulous shape in the yard covered with a tarp. "We brought up everything else you had left. Just a few little bottles, a funnel, a bunch of eyedroppers, and some dried plants and roots. You'd pretty much taken everything up North. What's left to pack up in the house?"

"I need to look through all the closets. I think we should take all the bedding. It'll be cold up north. Not much else is up there. Christmas decorations, I guess. But you never know what you might find. Earl never had a workshop or anything. He never was very handy. We always got a cousin to fix something or hired it out." She looked over at the truck. "It's hard to believe that a lifetime of living can be packed into the bed of a pickup."

"From what I could see from all those boxes in your library, it all won't fit into my truck."

Sephie let out a long, defeated sigh. "I'll go through the boxes again. It seems this house won't let go of us."

Floyd reached across Sephie to pat her hip. "I've been thinking about that. It will get really crowded in my truck with the three of us, going all that way. We need to rent a truck."

"That's too expensive!" She sat up further in the lounge. "We've been spending money right and left here. Or you have. Going out to eat and paying for gas and groceries."

"I have it at the moment. At least a healthy credit card. Yolanda talked me into getting one for emergencies before she went off to flight school. I just never used it or only enough to keep it active."

"As soon as the house sells, we're paying that thing off! And we'll bank the rest and keep that for emergencies. I still have Earl's pension. We can live off that. It's enough."

"Then we'll rent a small truck, and James can have his privacy. You can take turns keeping him and me company if you want." Patting her hip once more, Floyd rose and turned to look at the view as the sun came out, burning off the fog. Activity from the construction project on the opposite mountain drew his attention.

Sephie threw off the quilt and hoisted her aching bones upright. She stood beside him, watching trucks rolling up and down the new road up there.

"I think you'll get more than you expect from this house," Floyd announced. He swiveled his head to look at Sephie. "You'll be just fine."

She laced her am around his. "We'll be just fine."

The faint sound of "Ripple" could be heard inside the house from an open window.

"That your cell?"

Sephie didn't rush to grab it. She's learned that you didn't need to do that anymore, not like back when this house was built. You never knew who was on the other line. The old woman moved slowly as her joints and muscles warmed up. By the time she'd found where she'd left her phone in the kitchen, it had stopped ringing. Picking up the gadget, Sephie's eyebrows raised at what the caller ID told her.

Floyd had followed her inside and began pulling out eggs, butter, milk, and bread to make French toast. Turning to her, he asked, "Who was it?"

"B.D." she said. Not waiting to check on whether he left a voice message, she immediately dialed him. "What's he calling so darn early for?" When his Louisiana drawl reached her ear, she demanded, "What's wrong?"

"That's what I was going to ask you."

"What do you mean?" again Sephie demanded.

"Papa Mamoud called, got me out of my bed and now I'm wide awake. You know how hard it is to find him in the bayou. I didn't think he'd call back until the weekend. But he'd walked five miles until he'd gotten a ride into town to my auntie Bebe's house to use her telephone. Nearly took ten years off her life when he showed up at that hour, he did."

"What did he want?"

"That's just it," B.D. said. "He told me that the spirits kept him up all night, and that he had a message for that conjure woman I knew where I was. It took me a bit to figure out who he meant — that store owner who dabbled in hoodoo? He said, no, it was that real conjure woman, the old woman who knew herbs. How in the world he knew about you, I haven't a clue. I never told him."

"I'm no conjure woman. I don't mess with dark stuff."

"No, Miz Sephie, you don't understand."

Sephie's frown increased as she finally pulled out a kitchen chair and sat down. "Let me put you on speaker. Floyd's here, and he should hear this, too." She punched the button and put the phone on the table.

"Papa Mamoud made sure I understood. He says a conjure woman or man is someone who uses herbs or workings to help people. They sometimes combine local knowledge with their own people's lore — native or some other people's. So, you're a conjure woman." He took a breath and seemed to swallow something. "You're getting me sidetracked. Papa Mamoud told me that you're in danger. I figured something wasn't right from what Corinna told me. But Papa Mamoud said it was big mojo. And it was directed at you, not just your sister. I kinda gathered that some group had done a sending from what Corinna said, but it wasn't more than you could handle. Still, I wanted Papa Mamoud's protections for you."

"Big mojo? Was that all he said?"

"No." B.D. was silent for a while.

"B.D., you still there? Hello?"

"I'm here. It's just it's not just a group. Papa Mamoud thinks it's multiple sources, sending different things for different reasons. He said that there was a group sending to anyone connected to your sister. It's a sending to your entire bloodline, right down the line. Only blood."

"Are Mandy and Laura ok?"

"Sure. I found that odd. It's been quiet as a church here."

Floyd interrupted. "Mandy's not blood."

Sephie looked at him strangely. "Yes, she is."

"She's not even kin to your husband. Lige said his nephew's wife remarried and the man was a widower with a baby girl, Mandy. She's a Branscombe, not a Hill, and certainly not a Smith."

Sephie's brain was spinning. Family was family. "But-but—"

"It doesn't matter," B.D. interrupted. "We'll put protections on her here anyway. There's more. Papa Mamoud said there's a powerful working from powerful people, people with position and money. And somebody else who just doesn't want you there. Papa Mamoud said even the spirits of the land are pushing you out."

Floyd, who had paused whipping eggs in a bowl with a fork, stepped closer to the phone and asked, "Why would they do that?"

"I've always respected the land," Sephie argued. "I never took too much in my wildcrafting. I—"

"Papa Mamoud said you didn't belong there."

"B.D., I'm going. I'm selling and moving North."

"Guess I'll have to clean up the guest house. It's become a bachelor pad."

"Just for a little while."

"Oh? You going somewhere else?"

She looked up at Floyd. Neither one of them had told their families about their upcoming marriage. She wanted him to tell her to tell B.D., but he just stood waiting. She felt she should tell Mandy and Laura first; they were family — blood or not. A part of her also realized that once she let that news slip out of her mouth, it would be a reality; something she couldn't alter or take back. Staring at Floyd, she spoke. "Floyd's bringing a relative back to Fort Berthold; he's helping move my belongings. I'll only be in your space for about a week."

"A week? Why a week?"

"Floyd'll come back to get me then."

"Uh." B.D. sounded confused. "Okay."

Sephie shut her eyes. She was making a hash of things. Taking a deep breath, she finally blurted out. "Floyd and I are setting up housekeeping at his place on the reservation."

"Oh." He paused. "You say Yes yet?"

The old woman looked at Floyd. "Yes, I did. We're getting married in the Spring or Summer. But I haven't told Mandy and Laura yet."

The kitchen was filled with B.D.'s woo-hooing. Then, he

burst into a chorus of Three Dog Night's "Joy to the World."

Floyd just chuckled and returned to beating eggs.

"Who's that?"

They all turned to find James rubbing his eyes at the doorway to the kitchen.

"That's B.D." Sephie said, and then spoke to the phone. "James is looking for coffee. He's been helping us move. Was there anything Papa Mamoud said to do? Any kind of extra protections?"

"He told me you should wear a mojo bag. I'll tell you what to put in it. Maybe you all should wear one. It needn't be fancy. Just a cloth bag with herbs. And if you can find your cousin's shine to feed it, that would be best."

"Okay. Anything else?"

"He said he'd be doing a working for you. How long until you're on the road?"

Looking around the room, Sephie scanned the faces of the men. "Would Monday be too soon or not soon enough?" she asked B.D.

"Four more days." B.D. paused. "I'll tell Papa Mamoud. I'll see if Laura and Mandy will do a working, too. We might bring in everyone who helped before. And I'll put you all on church prayer lists for your safety. I think the sisters at St. Gertrude's might pray a novena for you. It will keep you protected while you travel."

"Always good to have all bases covered," Floyd said. "I'll call my church, too."

"And it won't hurt for us to spend our last day here at the two churches James plays at," Sephie said.

"James is a musician?" B.D. asked.

"A bluesman," Sephie said.

"Blues? Think he'd like to pause in Riverbend for a few days?"

Sephie chuckled. "You'd have to ask him. I think you're

getting as aggressive as Bill at snagging talent for The Watering Hole."

James, coffee mug in hand, leaned over the table where Sephie's cellphone lay. "Does it pay?"

"Not bad," B.D. said, "And he feeds you."

"Now, tell me what to put into those mojo bags," Sephie prompted.

Chapter 38

Day 11: Thursday, Lige's home,
deep in Dark Hollow, TN, late afternoon

"Y'all come back for another nip?" Lige said through a wheezy laugh as he stepped down from his porch onto his dirt yard to greet Floyd coming around the front of his pickup. "I may have to start charging." He offered his hand.

Floyd shook it, saying, "Not this time. I came to pick your brain."

"What for? My recipe?"

Emitting a chuckle, Floyd said, "I'm looking to buy a truck — cheap but roadworthy enough to get up to North Dakota. I was wondering if any of your clientele was wanting to sell."

"A truck?" Lige eyed the old Ford in his yard. "You havin' trouble with yourn?"

Shaking his head, Floyd said, "She's running fine. I need another one. Sephie has more stuff than I can transport safely in mine. I looked at renting a U-Haul for James, my cousin, to drive back, but I'd have to go into Knoxville to rent one and the expense. . . ."

"So, you want to buy one. Think that'd be cheaper?"

"Well, it might be if somebody had one they wanted to sell cheap."

Lige rubbed his stubbled jaw, thinking. "There are a couple o' guys, but they have recent models and just want to upgrade. Nobody's hurtin' for money that they'd want to sell cheap."

"Well, if you hear of anyone," Floyd said.

"When y'all fixin' to leave?"

"Monday."

Lige whistled. "Y'all ain't gonna find a truck by then." Looking past Floyd at a falling down old barn on his property, he frowned.

"Well, thanks, anyway, Lige," Floyd said and offered his hand.

"Hold on," Lige muttered, ignoring his hand. "I might have something." He waddled toward the old building and struggled with the huge double doors.

Floyd offered his muscle, and the two of them finally swung them open. The dark interior was cluttered with the detritus of decades of living and putting aside for a rainy day. Way in the back, with piles of clutter all around it, a hulking red and white Ford pickup truck sat on its haunches like a giant aging cat waiting to leap out for its final romp with equally aging mice. Floyd surveyed the beast, rubbing his hand over the county volunteer department logo on the doors.

"Not any rust," Lige commented. "I bought it at the police and fire auction about ten year ago. Thought Richard and Pollard would come into the business on the side and do deliveries for me. They didn't have any interest." He continued as he opened the hood. "I don't make as much product anymore and, well, people come to me now. It's just safer."

Floyd looked inside the hood and raised an eyebrow at the pristine innards of the truck.

"The guy who drove it had it all tricked out for high performance and speed. He told me it might help in my line of work. He just wanted to get to a fire real quick, though he only hauled backup equipment. So, the engine's in good shape. Course you'll need to get new tires. These have been sitting too long."

Turning from the engine to the fat man, Floyd asked, "How much?"

"Well," Lige began cagily, putting the hood down. "Seein' as how you're family now and you're taking our Sephie up into that cold country, how about. . . ." He paused for full effect, noticing Floyd tense in anticipation. "How about I just give it to you as a weddin' present?"

"I can't have you do that. Let me pay you something."

"Trust me, just clearing a path to get it out of this barn will be payment enough. And I might ask you to take a load to the landfill."

Offering his hand, Floyd said, "It's a deal."

Lige grinned as he shook his hand. "I'll go find the title and sign it over. I expect you'll register it up North, but you'll need a temp to travel." He reached into the bib of his overalls and pulled out a pocket watch. "If you hurry, you can get 'er done today."

"I'll get James out here tomorrow to move stuff, and we'll make that dump run."

"Sounds like James is a good 'un."

"He is indeed. Like you."

Chapter 39

Day 12: Friday, Sephie's house,
Dark Hollow, TN, late afternoon

Sephie shook her head as she brought two glasses of ice-cold lemonade into the driveway to the two men standing in front of the old truck, gleaming now from their effort, that was parked close to the porch. She was careful not to trip over the long extension cord that now was draped over the railing. They had used it to plug in her hair dryer to remove the volunteer fire department logos on both doors before giving the old heap a good scrub. But before that, the men had argued over whether Butter Wet Wax was better than Megular's Carnauba Wax before they washed the pickup. Floyd had finally grinned, slapped James on the back, and let the young man use the fancy Butter Wet Wax. They stood now, wiping their hands on blue garage rags like two teenagers with their first car.

"You boys ready for a hot date in that thing?" Sephie teased, offering them the lemonade.

"You up for some parking out on the back forty?" Floyd countered.

"Back forty? Where'd you come from? Round here you're rich if you got ten acres, some chickens, and a milk cow. Parking would be out on some dirt national forest access road."

"Well, are you game?"

Sephie punched his arm while James chuckled, enjoying the cold lemonade and their good-natured bickering.

Turing to the truck, Floyd said, "Well, the old girl has new shoes and is licensed so maybe this young one over here should take her out dancing." He reached into his jeans pocket and dangled two keys from a long black object.

James took the keys into his hand and started fiddling with the attachment, pulling out a variety of small tools. "A Leatherman mini! Where'd you find it?"

"At the auto store where we got the new tires and the wax."

"This is really cool!"

Floyd gave Sephie an incredulous look. "The boy finds more pleasure in the key chain and not the truck he's given."

There was silence and then James sputtered, "What? What?"

Giving James a slap on the back, Floyd said, "You've earned it. Just get Miz Sephie's belongings safely to her new home."

"I don't know what to say."

"Thank you is appropriate," Sephie said. "Now, go get cleaned up for your show tonight. I'll have supper ready by then."

Beaming, James gushed, "Thank you!"

Turning from watching James rush into the house, Sephie looked up at Floyd. "That was very generous of you."

"Well, I probably should've asked your permission first. After all, it was a wedding present for the both of us."

"I've got a station wagon in North Dakota," she said.

"And I've got a truck. Besides, that rebuilt high-performance engine will earn him creds with his cousins and may be get him a girl."

"I think he's got a girl." Sephie looked around at the lush mountains around them. "But would she trade all this and her people for a flat, cold place."

"You are. Think she's any different?"

Looking him frankly in the eye, she said, "Yes. She's close to her people." She paused. "Like you and James are."

"But we both left to follow something. We're finding our way back home."

"With Tennessee women?" She harrumphed.

Smiling, he sipped his lemonade.

Chapter 40

Day 12: Friday, Sephie's house,
Dark Hollow, TN, early evening

Spread out on the kitchen table were three bits of pure white cloth tied with twine. Floyd, James, and Sephie stared at them. Dinner had been eaten and cleared away. The only remnants were glasses of lemonade.

"They don't look like much," the old woman said. "I figured white was the best color for protection. I doubled the fabric so nothing would leak out, and I sprinkled the mix inside with Lige's butterscotch liquor. Y'all gonna smell like candy." She looked at the men. "Thanks to you both, I had all of the herbs and spices that Papa Mamoud told me to use. He asked for some stuff that you can't find easily, but I had it here. Like High John the Conqueror root. I'd taken some up North. B.D. used that in the three mojo bags he made up there for himself. This is shaved into the bag. From what B.D. said it'd be better off used whole, but the thing's so dang big. This'll have to do. I prayed over them and smudged and salted them. You both can do whatever you do to add your energy."

She handed one to James. "I'd suggest putting that close to you as possible. Against your skin would be best. But these aren't pretty enough to wear around your neck. A pocket maybe where you won't lose it. But I'd be careful putting it near your privates. High John the Conqueror can be used in love spells." She narrowed her eyes. "Being a musician attracts women anyway. You don't need any more charisma."

James took the bag, squeezed it in his hand, and sniffed it for a minute. He put it into his chambray shirt pocket which had a button to close it.

Floyd picked up his and put it into the pocket of his jeans, while Sephie turned slightly to stuff hers inside her bra.

"Are you coming to see me play tonight?" James asked.

"Yes, sir," Floyd said. "We've heard you here, but it's not the same as being in front of a live audience."

"Are you picking up Miss Corinna?" Sephie asked.

He smiled, lowering his eyes, but didn't answer.

"Well, then," Sephie said. "You can sleep in your own truck tonight since the consignment store took your bed away."

"I didn't need it anymore," he said. "The truck's just fine."

"Pretty lumpy sleeping with all those ribs in the truck bed."

He shrugged. "I'll figure out something."

"Take a cushion off of one the chaise lounges on the porch," Sephie suggested. "I wouldn't let the consignment shop take them. I wanted them for up North to look at the sunsets."

Floyd put his arm around her. "James, I may need you to help me build a screened porch at my place. There'll be more work for you until you find something permanent. I also need to pay you for your work here before we leave."

James held up his hand. "No. You gave me a place to stay and food. And the truck. I can't take any money for that. Besides, I'll get tip money tonight and some of the offerings from the churches on Sunday. I'll have food money. Will you be going to services with me?"

Floyd looked at Sephie.

"Just the Methodist church," she said. She looked up at Floyd. "Aren't you going to go to Mass before we leave?"

"Church is church," he said. "Besides, the Methodist church has such a lively service."

The old woman smiled. "Now, you run along, James," she said. "It takes this old lady a bit to get ready."

Chapter 41

Day 12: Friday, Connie's Bar and Grill,
East Hollow Gap KY, evening

The restaurant was packed as Sephie and Floyd were led to the table where Corinna sat with a glass of red wine and the remnants of a salad. Taking their seats, they quietly greeted the young pharmacist and quickly gave Millie their order of iced tea, white wine, and a cheese tray. Over the stage, a handmade banner read Farewell Show, casting a slight shadow over James who was bent over his guitar, his hat masking his face, as he noodled on the guitar.

Floyd found guitar blues much like bluegrass music; over time, it began to sound like one long unending song. James was good, no doubt. But his noodling was more like lounge piano, background to the hub of people's conversations. Yet, here they were, packed into every seat, eating and enjoying themselves, only half listening.

When Millie brought their wine and iced tea, she smiled at the stage. "Gonna miss that boy," she muttered in a husky voice.

As James finished the song, the audience, noticing a gap in the soundtrack of their lives, stirred to applaud politely. The musician raised his head and pulled a microphone on a stand closer to his mouth as he muttered his thanks. Looking around the room, he spotted Corinna and the old couple, giving them a subdued smile. "This is my last night here, folks. It was good of you all to come out." He tuned a few strings and then said. "I'm going home. I've been away too long."

He launched into a slow, more rockish number from some British movie Floyd had seen a while back. Then, James —

179

surprise — broke into actually singing a homesick blues song by Jerry Jeff Walker and then an upbeat B.B. King tune about going home to see his baby. He ended the set with "Sweet Home Chicago," but he replaced Chicago with New Town.

After the applause, James put his guitar in its stand and stepped off the stage, heading for their table. Corinna, smiling, slid over to make room for him.

Up on the stage, a very large woman with bottle red hair teased high into an 80s do and dressed in a flowered mumu stepped to the microphone. "Y'all know me. I own this place so y'all better drink up — but behave yourselves." She laughed and the audience did, too. "If I'd known that boy could sing," she said, "I'd have made him stay. But his mama misses him. He's been gone too long. He needs to get up North where it'd freeze the balls off a pool table, I hear." The audience laughed. "So, dig deep into your pockets when the tip bucket goes around and help this blues man get home."

Floyd looked over at James who was looking down at the table humbly. At that moment, Millie came by and placed a beer in front of the musician and the cheese tray in front of Sephie and Floyd.

"You'll get food money and then some," Floyd said quietly, picking up a slice of cheese.

"I didn't know you could sing," Corinna commented.

"I'm not very good. But sometimes you don't need it for blues. I'd rather just play."

"Ever think about doing duets?" Floyd asked.

"I don't have a voice for harmony," he said.

Sephie screwed her face up at Floyd. "What're you plotting, old man?"

He just shrugged. "Music is a big part of James' life. He's going home but there's not much going on around New Town."

"But isn't Bismarck close by?"

He nodded. "Yeah, but don't we know where there are opportunities, and he might break in closer to Riverbend."

"You got this all planned out, old man." She harrumphed and sipped her glass of wine.

"What're you talking about?" James demanded quietly.

"Your credentials can benefit a friend who's a very versatile singer. He sings in churches, too, and has a regular gig at a restaurant. He's playing with a guy now, but I think you two might be a better fit. He does some theater as well. They might need a guitarist in a pit band."

"Who're you talking about?"

"B.D.," Floyd said and took a drink from his glass of tea.

"The guy with the voice?"

"Yep, the guy with the voice," Sephie said. "Y'all should see him call the birds. Strangest thing. He has this affinity with them."

"What I can see is this, James," Floyd said. "You can spend most of your week back home with your family and then drive into Riverbend on Thursday and stay with B.D. Then you can rehearse and you and B.D. can play at The Watering Hole like on a Saturday. You might be able to get a gig at the VFW on a Friday. Both of you can then play in churches on Sundays. If B.D. gets into another play or knows of one that needs a guitar player, you can stay longer for that. All I ask is that you come play for my church once in a while. I've got B.D. coming sometime to sing for us."

Shaking his head, James said, "You do have this all figured out."

"You'll be coming back as a national touring musician playing in Riverbend, not a boy coming home because you didn't make it big."

"It's all in the spin," Corinna said, before finishing her glass of wine. "So, you're leaving on Monday?"

Floyd looked at Sephie. "Barring something happening, maybe Sunday after church."

"I've got to disconnect the phone and the electric and gas tomorrow before the offices close at noon," Sephie said. "And talk to my bank about transferring my account to North Dakota. Then we start packing the trucks. I do have the last kitchen things to box up so we'll probably eat sandwiches from then on."

A panicked look passed over James' face, causing him to look at Corinna who was studying her empty wine glass. "But, I—"

"You know you're welcome to visit, Miss Corinna," Floyd said.

"And my great-niece Mandy and her wife Laura would love to pick your brain about healings that you do," Sephie said. "They have a shop in Riverbend where they sell my tinctures and salves."

Corinna raised her head and brightened. "I'd like that."

"B.D. lives next door to the shop," Sephie added. "That's where James will be staying on those long weekends." She turned to him. "If you and B.D. can work things out." She leaned back against the booth cushions. "I can't imagine a musician or a singer not playing or singing. The Divine gave you both talent that must be used. B.D. found that out in Riverbend. You might, too."

With a brief glance at Sephie, Floyd said, "We're going to call it an early night. Miss Corinna, could you come over tomorrow evening for supper? I'd like you to bless the trucks before we leave on Sunday."

The young woman smiled. "I'd be honored to."

Chapter 42

Day 12: Friday, Sephie's home,
Dark Hollow TN, late evening

From the bathroom, Sephie shuffled into the bedroom in her soft slippers. She sat down on the edge of the bed and began to brush her hair. Each stroke was purposeful as she smoothed out the snarls the day's labors had produced in her hair. Though she had straightened her hair before they had gone to Connie's, she felt her hair, and perhaps herself, needed more chastisement. Applying a healthy yank, she uttered a soft cry, and it wasn't from the force of her hairbrush, which she threw on the bed.

"I've tried to be respectful," she lamented at Floyd who stood buttoning his pajama shirt. "I harvest only a few leaves or flowers from each plant. I make sure I only take one or two whole plants from any one place. And I don't glean from the same area until two years have passed so the plants can rejuvenate and multiply. And I always thank the plants themselves and any spirits there. How can Papa Mamoud think the land is displeased and attacking me?" She pleaded mournfully.

Floyd quickly moved to stoop in front of her. Taking her hands, he pulled them together and said, "The spirits of the land are disturbed. You see what's being done on the far mountain and on others."

"It was the strip mining first, and then the government made them reclaim the land and replant it."

"But it didn't really help, did it?"

She shook her head sadly. "No, those of us who've been here a long time remember what it was before. Spraying some grass seed couldn't cover up the gash in the top of those mountains. And then there was the flooding and waste from the mining."

"Now the coal companies have moved on to other mountains," Floyd said, "and the developers moved in. They can use some of those blasted mountain tops to build on, but they want places that have beautiful views, like you have."

"Except now, all I'll be able to look at is the new resort community over yonder."

"A gated community. People with money who don't appreciate what the locals cherish." He kissed her hands. "I think that your sister was the least of the reasons you spent so much time in your cabin and in the hollow gleaning wild plants. I think you were trying to preserve this mountain through your knowledge."

"And I will leave all that behind now," she admitted, defeated. "I can't save the whole mountain. And there won't be any of those medicines up North."

Floyd smiled. "You'd be surprised what grows up North. You need to connect with some of the ladies at my church whose Grannies still go out and harvest. There are different medicines there and some are the same. And I think B.D. can get you the more exotic things from the bayou. You have connections now. You can still make your medicines and share your knowledge. I bet Mandy and Laura would like you to teach classes at their shop."

Sephie smiled. "Mandy mentioned that, but we got distracted by all the strange happenings up there."

"There'll be time to do that now. And you'll eventually share what you learn from my people. Knowledge can protect the old ways and can protect the land. You'll teach respect and ethics."

She nodded.

Floyd released her hands, stood, and picked up the hairbrush. "Enough of this. You'll pull all of your hair out." He put it on the bedside table with the sole lamp left in the house.

Sephie got up and shuffled to the other side of the bed near the open window as Floyd got in on the side by the door. When she was tucked beside him, he turned the light off and cradled her in his arms. "You need the peace out at my place."

"What's it like in New Town?"

"Well, we do have a casino and there is Lake Sakakawea, the second largest manmade lake in the country. And there is still some boomtown mining activity going on in the region."

"Boomtown? So, you have your own land issues."

"Yes, and the people aren't immune to the lure of corporate dollars. But my house is on the northeastern edge of the reservation. It's a little rolling out there, not quite as flat as the area around Riverbend. It's green in the summer. There is some wheat farming near me, but I'm no farmer. I only grow vegetables around my house. You can walk and sometimes see bighorn sheep and deer out on the land. They imported the sheep, but the deer have been on the rez for generations. And pronghorn antelope."

"Where the deer and the antelope roam, huh?"

Floyd chuckled. "Yep. There always seems to be a slight wind out there because it's so flat. You can hear the meadowlarks in the morning. They have such a sweet song. And in the evening if you're near water, you can hear loon song."

"Any katydids like those outside?" Sephie asked, listening for a moment at their night music.

"No, I'm afraid not. But, again, if you're near water, you can hear frogs."

"That'd be nice. Birds and frogs. And seeing antelope."

"I walk the land as much as I can to get away from the wild west in town. That's why I think James would benefit from B.D.'s influence and his musical opportunities. Riverbend is a city, but it's not been infected with oil boom fever. It's all the way over on the eastern side of the state. Far, far away."

"Is it that bad?"

185

"It's better now since the boom is fizzling. Global oil prices dropped a few years back and production slowed. I remember a home health nurse in Riverbend, a young Black woman, telling me one summer solstice that she was out doing a home visit in New Town when the boom first started. She said as she drove into town, it felt like stories she'd read about the gold rush in California. She found her motel and literally barricaded herself in her room for the night. She actually put a chair under her doorknob. In the morning, she made it out into the country to the family she was serving and then took an alternative route back to Riverbend. It's a whole lot tamer now."

Sephie pulled Floyd a little closer. "I don't think I'd feel safe either."

"But the land remains and still offers peace. It forgives. It will know your heart, Sephie, and it will accept you."

Chapter 43

Day 13: Saturday, Sephie's home,
Dark Hollow TN, evening

As Floyd set the table, Sephie put a huge bowl into the oven at a very low temperature to warm. The old woman groaned as she straightened and surveyed the room. The only things left to pack were what she'd used to make and serve dinner. The coffee pot and coffee would remain on the counter until after they left for church in the morning.

"You overdid it, old woman," Floyd chided.

"Then ply me with ibuprofen and a gentle massage when the young people leave." She narrowed her eyes at him as she noticed him flexing his right arm up and down as if it ached. "Looks like you might've overdone it, too."

"We'll both have ibuprofen and massages then."

"Glad there's no furniture to slam around." Sephie giggled.

"Old woman, I'm too tired to even think about that."

Sephie moved over to his side and put her arms around him. "Doesn't matter. We'll sleep soundly." She sighed. "I never noticed until I talked to B.D. the other day, but the energy here is sluggish."

"With all the slamming and witch balls and whirlwind exorcizing?"

Craning her neck up to look at his face, she said frankly, "Yes. Even with James and Corinna's energy here, it's—"

"Not like up in Riverbend?"

She shook her head. "I mean we had a lot going on that we were trying to figure out up there, but the space was safe. Both

187

spaces. The store and the little house. There was a community there. In such a short time, we made friends."

"Are you worried that when we get to Fort Berthold, the energy will be gone?"

She smiled ruefully. "You mean the thrill will be gone?"

He merely raised an eyebrow.

She shook her head. "Not between us. But there will be new challenges that I haven't a clue how I'll handle. It's just that James needs to be around all of that energy in Riverbend. He needs it."

"You do, too. We'll visit often. It's only about four and a half hours away."

Smiling, Sephie admitted. "You're right. I got closer to Mandy and Laura when I was back there. I miss them. I think we validated one another, appreciating what we know and who we are. For the first time in a very long time, I wasn't criticized for my knowledge and for the work that I do."

"And they were accepted by family for being who they are. Being other-gendered is normal for my people and most native groups. I think that was one of the first points of acceptance we had between us. Then, they appreciated the spiritual goods I made for them."

Sephie squeezed his middle. "You and I can ease into our twilight years slowly, contemplatively out there on your property." She squinted at him and teased, "Do you have a back forty?"

He smiled and kissed her. "I own a section, part on the rez and part off."

Stepping back, the old woman said, "A section?" She tried to figure out just how much land that was. "Isn't that—"

"640 acres. So, yes I have a back forty." Floyd moved to a drawer to pick out silverware. "It's been in my family for generations. I almost lost it once when I couldn't pay taxes on it. But I finally scraped it up with late fees." Beginning to place forks and knives alongside plates, he warned, "When we get back home, when you mention that your family farmed here, don't be surprised when they ask you how many sections your daddy had."

Her mind was spinning. "I wasn't kidding about what I said about being rich was owing ten acres. Earl was considered rich because we bought these forty acres and built a new house. We weren't really, just comfortable enough not to have to worry about paying a mortgage and putting food on the table. Earl was a good provider, and I didn't have to work outside of the home."

"I'm not rich. I'm land poor," Floyd said. "Life is hard on the rez, but it's where our ancestors are and family is. And it's too flat and the wind blows too much for any energy to be stagnant." He smiled. "I think you'll like it there."

The sound of the front door banging and laugher floated in from the living room.

"Better get these mountain beans into a bowl," Sephie said. "Simple fare but something I grew up on. Mountain beans with pork and potatoes served with a big dish of pickled beets." She sighed. "I will miss Agnesia's canning."

"I can get you a new pressure canner, safer than that monstrosity your sister had that I carted to the dump. And some of the ladies from church could come help you. If you'd help them with their canning."

"It sounds like your church ladies will be busy with me. Are you pawning me off on them?"

He kissed her one more time. Staring deep into her eyes, he said with a smile, "Never."

She smiled, finally beginning to relax into the dream of a new life with Floyd.

Chapter 44

Day 13: Saturday, Sephie's home,
Dark Hollow TN, late in the evening

The sage smoke wafted over the cargo, tarped and tied down with extra-long bungee cords, on James' truck. He was carrying the dishes, other kitchenware, and the bedding, as well as most of the books Sephie had pared down from her library. Floyd's truck held the propane fridge, remnants from Sephie's herbs, the framed pictures, two bookcases, the bureau, and extra clothes and odd bits tucked into the drawers. The chaise lounge cushions protected the bookcases and the bureau and the lounges themselves had been slid between them. All that, too, had been tied down, then tarped and secured with bungee cords.

Corinna had smudged every inch of both truck cabs and now the outsides of both of them. She even managed to urge some smoke underneath with a feather and had asked both men to open the hoods to bless their engines.

While she smudged, Floyd sang a chant and used his rattle. James had found a metal garbage can lid and a stick and kept time on his makeshift drum. Sephie just stood and prayed for a safe journey.

Corinna stepped away from the truck and dowsed the burning end of the sage smudge into the dirt of the driveway. Floyd and James ceased their ministrations as the young woman nodded solemnly. "That felt right," she said.

Floyd reached into his shirt pocket and pulled out a folded piece of paper. He handed it to Sephie. "I wrote this out for you. You can put it into your own words."

Sephie read over what he'd written and noted the sequence and what needed to be said. The old woman folded it up again and handed it back to Floyd, nodding. She turned to look at her house, lit up in the fading light. She noted the dark shapes of the mountains in front of the house, lit with work lights and trucks continued to move up and down the winding road there. She took in the long driveway of her property and the path that led down the mountain into the hollow where her empty cabin stood. Turning her head to the sky, she noted the faint stars trying to come out and the full moon that made that more difficult. Finally taking a deep breath and spreading her arms wide, she began.

> "We call upon the spirits of this place and of this southern land
>
> To be at peace with us as we leave.
>
> We call upon the spirits of rivers and creeks, mountains, hollers and gaps
>
> To be at peace with us as we leave.
>
> We call upon the spirits of plants and all sacred wild and growing things used for our benefit: Beauty, healing, spiritual uplifting, protection
>
> To be at peace with us as we leave.
>
> We call upon the spirits of birds and animals and all living things
>
> To be at peace with us as we leave.
>
> We thank you for your blessings."
>
> Then she added from her heart, "I love this place, but I just want to make a home somewhere else."

Letting her arms fall to her side, Sephie humbly bowed her head. After a few seconds of thanks, she felt a tingling along her arms and the sense of others, more than just those beside her. She raised her head to see a mist rise from the woods on both sides of her dirt driveway. Figures emerged from the darkness into the mist, even a couple rising from the dirt far down the driveway. There were shapes of men and women; some dressed as her mountain ancestors in overalls and worn hats and flour sack dresses and sunbonnets; some in buckskin and feathers and beaded cloth. A stag with a many-pointed rack stepped onto the dirt drive and stared at them. Smaller animals ventured out gathering around the stag's legs. Other creatures emerged from the undergrowth, glowing with energy, having the shapes of plants: ginseng, goldenseal, may apple, Saint John's wort, and even High John the Conqueror. Two trees, one on each side of the drive seemed to shake themselves and began to give off a fluorescent glow. An owl and a hawk fluttered in and sat on a limb of each tree; the owl on the left and the hawk on the right. A few lightning bugs danced above the figures, intermittently emitting their yellow lights as a sparkling dance for those gathered below them.

Sephie heard Corinna catch her breath and she saw from the corner of her own eye that the young woman had reached for James' hand. Sephie didn't want to take her eyes from the gathering of these spirits but wanted to gauge Floyd's reaction. She needn't have worried. He had silently moved behind her and put his hands on both of her shoulders, solid, protective, ever present.

A song began to rise from deep inside her and began to rumble in her throat. It wasn't a song from her ancestors nor an echo of Floyd's high-pitched singing that was almost a lamentable cry. It was something she had learned at the Summer Solstice Festival that Mandy and Laura had organized where she had first met Floyd. Out of her mouth the words emerged: "We all come from the mother and to her we shall return."

Floyd added his tenor once Sephie had finished one round. Then, James joined in and finally Corinna. They sang the brief verse through six times, with the last one embellished with harmonies. Sephie smiled as she ended the song, enjoying the pleasant surprise of finding each of them had managed a different part.

The old woman's ancestors had screwed their faces up not quite understanding what was being sung, though some of the women finally moved their heads into a knowing nod, being mothers themselves. The native figures offered reserved smiles. As the song progressed, the animals and the plant spirits moved slightly closer to the humans, attentive, listening. The big stag flicked an ear once, then twice but not at some pestering mosquito or fly. It was more like a faithful dog listening, but there was wisdom there, older, profound, inscrutable.

Sephie watched, muttering, "Herne, we are honored." She was unsure from where those words had come. But they sounded right and respectful. Then she bowed low from her waist.

When she straightened, the mist rose higher around the figures obscuring but not impeding their backwards retreat into the woods that had become visually impenetrable in the deepening night.

Sephie bent again, but this time she touched her palms to the earth in a reverent gesture. Floyd did the same. James watched them and copied their actions with Corinna following suit.

The old woman looked up at Floyd when she had straightened. "I don't think the spirits of the land were a problem though Papa Mamoud said they were."

Floyd frowned. "Papa Mamoud said the spirits knew you didn't belong here anymore. They know your heart, that you love this land and have been respectful, and that you are leaving. They honored you by appearing and you gave them honor." He looked down the dark road. "But they will be a problem to the developers who buy this property. And they will buy it."

Sephie merely nodded, resigned to progress and greed, suddenly feeling weary beyond measure. "I think I need my bed," she said. Turning to Corinna, she opened her arms and enveloped the young woman in a hug. "Thank you, my dear, for all of your help. Please come North and visit us. You're family now." She smiled.

"I will, Miz Sephie."

To James, the old woman said, "I've never really thanked you for your open-mindedness about all this. It isn't something many young people know about or can handle." She smiled at Corinna again and then said to James, "Make sure you get enough sleep to play in church and drive tomorrow."

Chapter 45

Day 14: Sunday, Grace Methodist church,
Dark Hollow TN, late morning

It had been a pleasant surprise to see Corinna in the front row pew at the Methodist church that morning when Sephie and Floyd arrived. She had craned her head as if to watch the back doors for them and waved them to the front. There was an air of festivity in the church as if it were celebrating something on this humid summer morning — well past Easter and school graduations. The only thing that came to Sephie's mind was maybe confirmation. Those schedules could be any time during the church calendar. And, indeed, that was verified when the minister took the pulpit.

"Good morning. I'm Elder Jackson for those of you who may be visiting today," he said. "Today's service has been crafted by the graduating confirmation class. They designed the litany, picked out the music, and are performing it with our usual young musician friends, and they even wrote the sermon. Holy Communion will be supervised by seminary students and our elders. Our offering this morning will go to one of our young musicians, James Redman, who will be leaving us today, making his way back to his home in North Dakota. So, when the offering plate comes around, please help get this young man back home to his mama."

The congregation tittered quietly as Elder Jackson left the sanctuary area and took a seat in the front pew across the aisle from Floyd.

A couple of new players with acoustic guitars occupied seats near James and the bass man who normally played these services. The piano player and drummer were also young teenagers. The guitars began with accomplished noodling on the piano to "Morning Has Broken." The congregation stood and sang heartily.

Sephie smiled at the choice. It was a song she'd heard in her younger years.

The service continued with scripture readings and then George Harrison's "My Sweet Lord" for the offertory. It was another good choice because it could be prolonged indefinitely as the metal baskets on long poles were thrust into every pew. When all was collected, the money was brought to the front where a young man prayed a blessing over it for James' prosperity and safe travels.

But it was the youngsters' version of "You Raise Me Up" before their sermon that caused Sephie to grip Floyd's arm. It began slowly with piano music and a solo male voice. A brief bridge was played by James on electric guitar. Then a young woman joined the male singer for a chorus before the whole confirmation class stood to add their voices to the song, adding a counterpoint to the two singing the melody. The song ended quietly with the male singer's voice acapella.

Tears streamed down Sephie's face, causing Floyd to shift in his seat to hand her his handkerchief. She smiled. "B.D. has to learn that song."

"We'll get James to teach him."

The sermon was presented by a young woman, who talked about what the song lyrics said. She pointed out how the parents of the confirmation class had raised them up. She talked about how her confirmation teachers had done the same. Then she stressed that God had also raised them up, stressing how that because of all of them, they all were more than they could be. It was a brief but moving lesson.

Holy Communion was distributed and for the first time in a long time, Sephie felt compelled to partake. It was different from what she'd remembered from old Baptist services and very different from the few Catholic masses she'd attended. And today's communion was even different from the service she was at last week. Instead of calling people forward, they passed a basket of freshly baked cornbread and biscuits that had been cut into pieces and a tray of small glasses. She knew that they all partook together so she held the sacraments in her hand and waited.

She was surprised when Floyd did the same. He simple muttered, "Same God."

Smiling, she heard one of the two young people at the pulpit speak about how the Methodist church includes everyone in communion. They then went on to read the communion service.

After the congregation as a whole put bread into their mouths and washed it down with grape juice, Sephie reached for Floyd's hand, still holding the small glass, while his other made the sign of the cross. She watched his lips mutter a silent prayer. In that brief moment, she felt bound to this man beside her more than if they had just completed an elaborate ceremony.

Then the congregation was on its feet, as a young person at the pulpit, prayed a benediction and the confirmation chorus and band dived into "Shine" by Collective Soul that started quietly and soon morphed into a very raucous metal tune with fuzzed electric guitars. And not just James' but another guitarist had traded his acoustic for an electric. Yet, it was James' full-blown rock out — though brief — that brought grins on the faces of the young people around him. He actually raised his head and grinned with them.

Sephie chuckled at the daring of the young people to bring heavy metal into a church. She also had a pang of regret for taking James' away. Those kids really liked him and, moreover, they respected him. She also wondered what kind of influence he'd have on the conservative churches B.D. sang in. But if he could play for a snake-handling revival and a regular Baptist church, he'd do ok.

It took a long time for James to say his goodbyes, not only to this congregation, but to Corinna as well. The boy had handed the collection baskets to Floyd and asked him to count it for him. He also reached into his jeans pocket and pulled out an envelope with a wad of bills inside that he added to the pile. "That's mostly ones. I feel like I've been a dancer at a club," he muttered before taking Corinna by the arm and into a side corridor.

Floyd chuckled as he moved to an empty pew in the back near the doors. He and Sephie separated the currency into denominations in order to count better.

"Mandy always just counts the number of bills in each stack," Sephie said, "and then figures out how much is there according to what they are."

"Always a good practice."

Once they had the money separated, they counted the number of bills in each pile. Sephie put that down on the back of the envelope the ones had been in. They'd actually found a ten and a five in there among the singles. After they had made all of their calculations, there was $300 in his haul, with half in ones.

Floyd pulled out some twenties from his own wallet and replaced the big pile of ones with them. "He can't go around with that wad in his pocket."

To Sephie, it looked like more than the value of the ones he handed to her.

"Put that in your purse. I'll put the rest of this into the envelope. Now let's see if we can urge James' to get on the road."

It took a little while longer but eventually James and Corinna came out of the church and found the old couple leaning against Floyd's truck. They were eating cold fried chicken legs and drinking from cans of soda. There was a cooler at their feet.

"You need to put that in your truck," Floyd said, pointing to the cooler with his drumstick. "It's got some cold chicken in there and stuff left in the fridge, along with cold drinks."

Reaching inside, James pulled out a plastic container. He opened the lid and offered the bowl to Corinna, who shook her head. Her eyes were troubled.

"I need to get on home," she said. "Y'all be safe on the road." She gave Sephie a hug but hesitated in front of Floyd.

"I've got sticky hands, child, but you can hug me," he said.

She did indeed and kissed his cheek. "Thank you," she whispered.

He tilted his head, not quite understanding.

Turning to James, she offered him a brief last kiss and turned to walk away down the sidewalk to where she's parked her car. The noon day sun made her black braid shine.

It was an awkward moment that tightened Sephie's throat. She gulped down some soda to loosen the lump.

Looking helplessly at the bowl of chicken, James muttered, "You made chicken this morning?"

"It was the least I could do while I did the bedding and packed up what there was left in the kitchen," Sephie said.

"Let's get this thing inside your truck," Floyd urged. "You can grab a couple of legs and a soda and get on the road."

Floyd put his soda can on the hood of his truck and Sephie stuffed a few sheets of paper towel into his jeans' pocket. The men then each took a handle and walked the cooler down the sidewalk to his truck, opposite where Corinna had gone. When they'd gotten there, Sephie saw them open the truck door, hoist the cooler in, and then Floyd reached into his shirt pocket for the envelope. There was some discussion and then Floyd returned to Sephie.

"Everything OK?" the old woman asked.

"It's probably a good idea he's driving by himself for a while. I told him where to meet us in Indianapolis. He'll put it the GPS on his phone, and he can take his time. He's got a radio in the truck and an adapter to charge his phone. He'll be ok. And he can call us. It isn't like when we were young and we didn't have cellphones to ask for help or just have company."

"I guess we should get to it then," Sephie said, stuffing the drumstick into her mouth and opening the door. She put the can of soda into the cup holder and then proceeded to haul herself inside with an assist from Floyd.

The old man retrieved his soda and got into the cab of the truck. He finished his drumstick and wiped his hands on a paper towel before turning on the ignition. "We'll all stay in a motel tonight, but we'll stop for dinner in Indianapolis. We can get an earlier start in the morning and maybe make it all the way to Riverbend before dark tomorrow. I wouldn't mind some of Bill's funeral hotdish by then."

Putting the truck in gear, he swung out of the parking space and headed up the road.

Sephie looked out her side mirror and saw a shiny red and white pickup pull out farther down the road behind them. It had begun. Another grand adventure.

"No regrets?" Floyd asked. It was said in jest but there was a definite question there.

She smiled and put her hand on his thigh. "No regrets." Then she added. "Just help me through the changes, Floyd."

He reached down, pulled her hand off his thigh, and kissed it. "Always."

Chapter 46

"Are we stopping tonight?" James said as he added black pepper to his hamburger at the restaurant north of Indianapolis. It was a small-town diner that offered comfort food.

Floyd was digging into a plate the size of a platter full of sliced roast beef and mashed potatoes covered in gravy. "Peoria," he said before stuffing another forkful of hot goodness into his mouth.

"You planning on finishing all that?" Sephie asked, frowning as she dipped a spoon into a cup of tomato and basil soup. That and her half of a club sandwich looked substantial enough.

"Afraid I'll get fat in my old age?"

"Afraid you'll keel over with a heart attack, old man," she said.

Changing the subject, Floyd asked James, "Hear anything good on the radio?"

He nodded. "Yeah. There's a song I want to learn. I'll have to look up the lyrics. I think I've got the melody down pretty much. It's simple enough."

"Did you get to keep the music from the church service today?" Sephie asked.

"I wasn't supposed to. But the confirmation kids had saved all of the music from the past few months I'd been there and put it into a folder for me. They said it was their last rebellious act." He laughed and shook his head. "That's rebellion? They all kicked in a few dollars to cover the cost and left it in the music director's office. I doubt those kids would even know how to push boundaries."

"They seemed like good kids," Floyd said.

"It was the biggest confirmation class they'd ever had. I think it's because the music at the services drew them there and they stayed. Music can be a real siren." He looked at Sephie. "Was there a special song you liked?"

She nodded as she wiped her mouth with a paper napkin. "'You Lift Me Up.' I want B.D. to learn it." She glanced at Floyd. "I think you and B.D. will do your own share of rebellion in drawing young people to church. And Floyd probably wants you to start overhauling his musical selections."

Looking surprised, Floyd protested. "I never said he could change the way I handle my choir. Besides, everything has to get approved by the priest."

"But it never hurts to add a fresh, youthful perspective," she argued. "You can't say that 'You Lift Me Up' wouldn't be inspiring for even the most conservative member."

"Well, it is a moving song. Some would say it's too secular." He thought a minute. "I heard a story about the former priest who pitched a fit because they used Bob Dylan's 'Good Shepherd.' That was back when everything had to be from an approved list."

"It wasn't Dylan," James said. "I think he might have performed it somewhere before. I kind of remember his gravelly voice singing the chorus. But it was by a rock group. Airplane something."

"Jefferson Airplane?" Sephie said startled. "In church?"

"The line was 'Oh good shepherd, feed my sheep,'" Floyd continued. "Done with the right voice it was actually a nice intro to the Eucharist, but you couldn't sing the full version. I did use it once as sort of a litany of confession and tinkered with the lyrics."

"And you're worried about me tainting your musical choices!" James grumbled.

"Let us reason together, my young friend," Floyd said gently. "Differences of opinion often breed wonderful creative outcomes. I expect you to keep challenging me. I suppose you'll even bring in a Robert Johnson or Muddy Waters tune into church sometime."

James grinned. "I accept your challenge."

"Uh-oh," Sephie muttered, giving her sandwich all her attention.

Floyd then turned toward Sephie, probably to change the subject again. "You should call Mandy and Laura about when we'll get there tomorrow. They think we're leaving then."

Reaching into her purse, she pulled out her phone and scrolled her contacts to find her great-niece's number. Punching the telephone icon, she waited as the phone rang.

"Aunt Sephie!" Mandy cried. "When are you going to get here?"

"Actually, we left this afternoon after church. We're in Indianapolis. We'll go a few more miles and then stop at a motel. It looks like we'll be there tomorrow night." She turned to Floyd. "What time do you think?"

Floyd thought a moment. "Around 8, I guess, if we can leave at 9 in the morning."

Sephie reported what he said to Mandy. "We'll need room in the back for two pickup trucks."

"No problem. I'll put my truck out front. How long can you stay?"

"I want to stay a few days. I miss you, Mandy-girl."

"How many beds do you need us to fix up?"

"Can Floyd and I have my old room? And James'll need a bed."

"Laura went over there today. B.D. picked up pretty well, though he'd sort of sprawled out all over the little house. She said it looked like a room at a frat house."

"Underwear hanging off the ceiling fan?" Sephie teased, and then saw James' eyes widen.

Mandy laughed. "Almost." There was a pause. "And so, it's official then? About you and Floyd?"

Sephie looked at the others at the table. "Yes, it's official."

"Did he give you a ring?"

"A ring?" She looked at the old wedding band Floyd had insisted she wear to her sister's funeral. She hadn't taken it off. "We haven't had time. But it's not necessary."

"It most certainly is! I'll have a talk with that gentleman when he gets here."

"Mandy, hold your horses. There'll be time to do all kinds of planning. It won't be until next year anyway."

"How'd cousin Debra take the news?"

Sephie coughed, realizing that she still hadn't made that phone call. Her phone beeped and she looked at it. "Mandy, I've got another call. I'll talk to you tomorrow from the road."

She swiped at her phone and said, "Hello?"

"Miz Sephie, I've got great news! I haven't even listed your house yet, but—"

"Who is this?"

"Stacy Singleton, your realtor, hon. Are you sittin' down? Well, I just sold your house!"

"You just sold my house," she repeated dumbly.

"Yes, hon! I got the most delicious offer from a developer out of Louisiana. He wrote a bid that's twice what you're asking for, with no inspection, and he's paying all of the closing costs."

"Twice the asking price?"

"Yes, ma'am! He wants the property that bad! So, can you come in tomorrow to sign the papers?"

"Uh, Miz Singleton, I'm on the road heading up North. Could you mail them to me? I can send you the address?"

"Mail? Honey, this man can't wait for snail mail. I'll email them to you and you can sign them electronically. What's your email address?"

"Email? I don't have an email address."

Floyd tapped her hand holding the phone and opened his hand. She let him take the phone but leaned in close to listen. "Miz Singleton, this is Floyd Whiteman. I'm Sephie's fiancé. Can you email those papers to me? We'll get a lawyer up in North Dakota to look them over and if it looks good, she can sign them electronically and get them back to you before the end of the week."

"The end of the week? I can't let this fish slide off the hook. If we wait too long, he will."

"Miz Singleton, if he's willing to pay double the asking price, he can wait a few days."

"I suppose."

"I realize you have a substantial commission coming, and it looks like you've earned every penny. Let me give you my email address. We'll look the contract over tonight, and we'll call you first thing in the morning if we want to move forward."

There was silence. "All right. I'll call you first thing in the morning."

Floyd gave her his email address and pressed the button to end the call. Handing the phone back to Sephie. "I may be land poor but you may be rich."

"What?" Sephie was confused. She hadn't really paid any attention to the price Stacy Singleton had put on the property when they first talked. But the realtor did know the property values in the area well.

"How much did your husband pay for those forty acres back in the 60s?"

"I think we got a mortgage for the land and then to build the house for about $50,000. That was a lot back then. The land wasn't worth much because it was so near the national forest and people thought the forestry service would just take that land anyway if it wasn't sold."

"Fifty thousand." Floyd shook his head. He looked at James. "You have any idea what property is worth in that area — just a house and an acre or two?"

The young man shook his head as he reached for his soda "Close to half a million dollars."

"Half a million?" Sephie sputtered.

"Yes, $500,000. I saw some properties for sale on my errands into town and then looked online. And you have 40 acres. If this developer is willing to pay double, with no closing costs, that's at least a million dollars. Of course, Miz Singleton will earn her five percent so you'll bank about. . . ." He calculated a moment. "About $950,000."

"Nine hundred—" she sputtered again. "How long can we live on that?"

"Very well on the interest alone for a long time."

Sephie fell back into her chair. "Well, I'll be."

Floyd's phone chimed. He pulled it out of his pocket and looked at it. "Got an email."

Sephie put her hand over his holding the phone. "I don't want to do this now. I need to get used to the idea."

He nodded and pocketed his phone.

Chapter 47

Eying James plate of pancakes, Floyd sighed. "I promise not to eat a heavy breakfast," he said. "I slept restlessly."

"I think it was that email on his phone that kept him awake," James suggested, pouring warm maple syrup over his stack of hot cakes.

"Probably," Sephie added, putting salt and pepper over her single egg. She picked up a half strip of bacon and said before popping it into her mouth, "I never thought you were a greedy old man."

"Curious, not greedy," he said, attacking a pair of over-easy eggs and hash browns. He'd also ordered a fat sausage patty.

"All right," Sephie conceded. "Look at your email."

Pulling out his phone, he called up his email account and opened the email. He read it quickly, scrolling through the message. "It seems Miz Singleton summarized the contract for you." He handed the phone to Sephie. While she read, he said to James, "She padded the asking price. I guess to give her room to barter down a client without losing her commission."

Sephie was trying to make sense of what she was reading. "It looks like there's nothing I'll have to pay, except Stacy Singleton's commission. She detailed that quite clearly. It's a lot. A lot more than you estimated. It's $150,000."

James raised his head from his mountain of buttery, syrupy goodness.

"Read on, Sephie," Floyd instructed. "Don't get lost in the details. Scroll down to the bottom. Look at the asking price."

She read the figures and then read them again. "Isn't that his offer?"

Floyd chuckled. "No, that's farther down. Read out what she says is the asking price."

"$1.2 million."

James choked on his last bite and reached for his coffee to clear his passageway.

Sephie scrolled down further.

"What does it say?" Floyd prompted.

"This can't be right."

"What's it say?"

"$2.5 million."

James laughed heartily and so did Floyd.

"What's so funny?" Sephie asked. "This is a typo."

"I think you need to call Miz Singleton and let her know you're considering it," Floyd said.

Looking up bewildered, she asked, "What could they possibly build there that's worth two million dollars."

"It's worth more than two million if that's what the developer's willing to pay. It's got to be a bigger resort community than the one on the far mountain," James said. "Maybe it'll be for Nashville stars or Hollywood actors. Does it matter? You knew that they'd develop it anyway even if you sold to a family. They'd offer them the money. It's better than selling to a coal or oil company."

"Only slightly better," she muttered.

"But," James began, his face curling into a frown. "It's a dry county. How're they ever going to keep celebrities there with no access to alcohol?"

Floyd took a thoughtful drink from his coffee cup. "When I was with the rodeo, we set up in a rodeo grounds near this tiny town. It was in the middle of a dry county. When I was having dinner one night after a show at the local café, I asked where the locals could get alcohol. The waitress pointed to the back counter. Among a lot of antique metal signs about food was a poster announcing the hours of a local private club. I asked her what were the requirements for membership. She said it was $100 a year for residents. Then she leaned in close and said that a local could bring a guest."

"And you were her guest?" James suggested.

Floyd cleared his throat and merely added. "They had a full bar."

"That's even legal?" James said.

"It was in Texas. Private clubs get different types of liquor licenses from the state. Each state is different. I suppose anyone with enough money and power could bring that little loophole to Tennessee."

"Oh lordy," Sephie said, "the spirits of the land will be so upset with me."

Floyd put his arm around her. "The spirits of the land will have to deal with this in their own way. They know your heart. You'll be shed of the troubles there and able to live as you please."

She searched Floyd's face. "I still haven't told Debra."

He pulled her close. "Tell her when you get to North Dakota. This isn't done until a lawyer looks at it anyway." Then he added. "And I'll call Yolanda tonight."

"Ripple" sounded and Sephie put Floyd's phone down to fish out her own from her purse.

"Hello?"

"Miz Sephie, did you get a chance to look at the offer?"

"Just a bit. We'll still need to have a lawyer look it over."

"Yes, but will you accept it?"

"Tell the developers that yes we will IF the lawyer says it's okay."

The sound of girlish screams and giggles filled Sephie's ear, making her pull the phone away from her head. When she put it back, Stacy Singleton was rattling away her gratitude.

Sephie interrupted. "We'll get into Riverbend late tonight and go find a lawyer tomorrow. If he says everything is okay,

I'll sign and get that to you. Shoot, maybe he can fax it to you all legal."

Again, a stream of giggles. Sephie couldn't bear any more and just said, "I'll call you tomorrow," and ended the call. "Well, that's that," she said.

Floyd nodded, returning to his breakfast. "We need to find a cutthroat lawyer."

Sephie screwed up her face. "We aren't fighting City Hall. What do you expect that lawyer to find in a contract?"

"Hopefully, not a thing. And you still have to call Debra."

"And you haven't called Yolanda."

"I'll do it in the truck."

"And so will I."

Chapter 48

Day 15: Monday, on the road
somewhere in Minnesota, afternoon

"At least she didn't scream at me," Sephie said bitterly, throwing her phone onto the space on the bench seat between her and Floyd.

"Came close though," he said. "I could hear her over the road noise."

Putting her head back onto her seat and closing her eyes, she said, "I need a drink."

"I'll buy you a big glass of wine at The Watering Hole tonight."

They traveled along in silence for a couple of miles as Sephie remembered Floyd's call to his granddaughter Yolanda. She was positively squealing with excitement. But her call to Debra wasn't as positive.

"What was she mad about the most? You selling or getting married?" Floyd asked.

"Somehow through the hillbilly grapevine she knew all about the sale of the house and land. Probably Stacy Singleton bragged to everybody about her big payoff and somebody called Debra."

"So, it was getting married. Does she think you're being disloyal to her dad?"

Sephie opened her eyes. "She thinks you're after my money. She didn't shut up until I told her you owned a section of land in western North Dakota."

"So, that's why you mentioned that."

"She somehow knew about the oil boom. Have I been

213

living under a rock? I didn't know about it or maybe I just ignored the national news."

Reaching for her hand, the old man said quietly, "I don't want to live off you."

"But a woman should live off a man?"

Glancing at her, he challenged, "Didn't you expect to? It's what our generation did."

"Look, Floyd, when we met, neither of us knew or cared about whether we owned anything." She glanced away and then admitted to him, "If you hadn't been persistent, I might've chased you."

He chuckled. "You could've fooled me. You were so hardheaded about us or the possibility of us."

"Yeah, well. I wasn't looking for romance. I don't remember how to court, not that I ever really did, and it felt—" Floyd waited, not wanting to fill in the unsaid words. "It felt foreign." There was a catch in her voice. "It didn't feel real."

Floyd pulled her hand to his lips and kissed it. "I'm not dirt poor," he admitted. "I never banked money when I was working the rodeo circuit. Even though I was a profligate, I did send money home regularly. My wife squeezed the life out of what there was. In fact, after she died, I found a bank book and she'd managed to put a little away, I figured for Yolanda. But I did bank her life insurance money. I've been doing jobs here and there, making spiritual goods, cooking at fairs and such. I've lived on that and social security. I pay my taxes. I keep the money in the bank for property taxes. I won't be holding my hand out to you."

Sephie looked at him, surprised. From his talk before about what a dissipated life he'd led on the rodeo circuit, she assumed he was only living on social security. She didn't have that because she never worked. She did have Earl's pension. That wasn't much, but it allowed her to do as she pleased with her herb work and maintain the house and pay property taxes.

"We're going to be married," she said finally. "We just have to work together and talk about major purchases. It sounds like you have some additions to make to your house, and we have a bed to buy."

"James and I need to build you a screened porch so you can watch the sunsets without mosquitoes. We're near a big lake. It's not like in Riverbend where the city sprays regularly. You'll have to wear repellant when we walk the land. And I think we need to add a room or a building for you to work with herbs and plants."

"Lots of changes," Sephie admitted. "I hope Mandy knows a good lawyer so we can get that all done before winter. Have you ever thought about keeping chickens?"

"People do," Floyd said. "But we'd have to heat the hen house if we wanted eggs all year or just raise them for the table during the season."

"Lots to think about."

Floyd squeezed her hand. "A future to plan."

Chapter 49

It was a pleasant summer evening, a least two hours before full dark, as Floyd and James parked their pickups behind Mandy and Laura's metaphysical shop, the North Star, and the little house where B.D. now lived. They had spent way too many hours in their vehicles that day, preferring to haul butt to get to Riverbend at a decent hour.

Sephie slid her stiff bones out of the truck and hobbled around it toward the back door of the shop. By the time she'd reached the first step, her body was moving smoothly. She and her companions mounted the steps and entered the back of the shop. Mandy and Laura hadn't taken down the big work table in the back where she had been preparing tinctures and salves when she'd gotten the call about Agnesia's passing. The lines of heavy twine they had strung over the workspace still bore bunches of dried herbs she hadn't handled yet.

Within seconds, Mandy, Laura, and B.D. burst into the back room from the main shop, enveloping Sephie and Floyd in hugs. Finally, separating from them, the old woman took James by the arm and brought him closer to the others. "This is James Redman."

There was a silence and then B.D. let out a guffaw, offering his hand. "Well, there's certainly no confusion about who you are," he said, as James shook hands with him. "Floyd had us scratching our heads. You're a relative of Floyd's?"

The young man nodded. "A cousin of sort of, but it's kinda hard to count."

"I hear you. Back on the bayou, I've got cousins coming out of the bald cypress, but it's hard to track down exactly who belongs to who and how far down the line they all are. Saying they're cousins is just simpler."

"Laura," Floyd began, "can you close up early? Let's move this party to the Watering Hole. I promised Sephie a big glass of wine."

"If I drank that now as tired as I am, I'd fall face first into my plate."

"Then let's get you some food and find a bed," Laura said.

It took only a couple of minutes for Mandy and Laura to lock the store. Then they all fled out the front and walked the short distance toward The Watering Hole. Mandy had commandeered Sephie and Laura had corralled Floyd. Sephie figured it was to pump each of them about wedding details. Behind them B.D. and James trailed in silence.

"So, did you tell cousin Debra?" Mandy asked.

The old woman could only shake her head. "She thinks Floyd's after my money."

"What money? You mean from the sale of your house? Floyd's a good guy. He has his own property."

"Yeah. Do you know a good lawyer?"

"Sure Phillip Anderson. His office is just around the corner here," she said as they waited at the cross street for a car to turn onto Third. "He handles all our legal work."

"A good guy? Honest?"

"Absolutely. And pretty ruthless when he's on your side."

"I don't need a shark. I just need someone to look over some papers and maybe give me some financial advice."

"Phillip is the man for you then."

Behind them, James was humming something that sounded like a folk tune, quite different from his usual blues or church fare.

"I know that tune," B.D. said. "I ran across it when I was

working on my final paper. It was lumped into both protest songs and environment tunes. Let me see if I remember some of the words — at least the chorus." From his mouth, came his rich baritone, singing about a grown son who wanted his father to take him back to the place of his childhood where paradise was, but the coal company had destroyed it, carrying it off by the truckload.

Pausing as they all drew up in front of The Watering Hole, Sephie turned back to B.D. "Rape of the land. But now it's developers," she said bitterly, feeling guilty about her own part in it.

B.D. screwed his face up not understanding and was ready to reply when James asked, "You been to Miz Sephie's place?"

"Well, sure, but—"

"They're building a big resort on the mountain facing her place."

He raised an eyebrow. "That mountain top was dynamited away for coal."

"Guess it's a new way to reclaim the land."

After plowing through the jungle of plants in the foyer, the party passed through the inner door to The Watering Hole. They were greeted by guitar music and some other plucked instrument at the hostess desk.

"What is that?" James asked.

Looking up at the water buffalo head mounted over the bar, B.D. said, "It's a Cape Verde water buffalo."

James looked confused. "No, I mean the music."

"Oh, that's Ali Farka Toure and Toumani Diabate. Guitar and kora. It's a funny instrument, looks like a big gourd with a long neck, and the strings are plucked."

"Got a picture somewhere?"

While they waited to be seated, B.D. fiddled with his phone, doing an internet search. He had just called up a photo when a big booming voice yelled, "Miz Sephie!" A big man with a walrus mustache approached them with his arms outstretched. His grin was infectious. "Sugar! Sugar, get out of that kitchen. Miz Sephie's back!"

As the man hugged Sephie tightly, a petite blonde woman rushed out from the back, trying to untie her apron.

When the man had released Sephie to shake Floyd's hand, Sugar beamed at the old woman, offering her a hug, too. She stepped back and sobered. "I was so sorry to hear about your sister."

"She's happy now," Sephie said. "She's been saying she's going to Glory for years. She finally made it."

"So, are you just finishing your visit or are you planning to stay?"

"I'm moving here. But—" she glanced up at Floyd. "But we'll be living at Fort Berthold."

Sugar looked at Floyd. "You finally asked her," she stated.

"I've been asking all along. She finally stopped stalling."

Sugar laughed and reached a hand up toward Floyd's face. He bent down to allow her to kiss his cheek.

"This calls for a celebration," Sugar gushed. "Just give me a minute, and I'll bring you an engagement feast."

"Don't trouble yourself, Sugar," Sephie said. "Anything will do. We're hungry and road weary."

"No worries," she said before the big man with the moustache took her elbow and pulled her away. "What's your hurry, Bill?" she protested.

He pulled her toward James and made introductions. "This young man just asked me if he can play here. I didn't even have to finagle him into it." Bill's face could have lit up the entire street. "I'm thinking he and B.D. ought to team up. What do you think, Sugar?"

"You handle all the entertainment. I just cook, remember?"

"But I appreciate your opinion."

"Whatever you want to do, dear."

Clapping his hands together and rubbing his palms, he said, "We need a big table and where to put it." He thought a moment, said, "Ah!" and yelled for two burly waiters to move two tables in an alcove into the back and bring out a big round one, which protruded prominently into the main dining room.

When the tablecloth was put on and the silverware placed, Sephie and her group pulled out chairs and sat down.

Bill then boomed out, "A glass of champagne for everyone, on the house. I have a special toast to make." He then leaned over the table and said in a low voice. "You get the good bottle and real glasses."

Grinning, he marched off to confer with the bartender.

Laying her napkin across her lap, Sephie said, "He shouldn't put up such a fuss."

"Enjoy it, Aunt Sephie," Laura said. "There will be many more celebrations to come."

"Where're the menus?" the old woman demanded. "I'm hungry."

Floyd just smiled before he said, "I think Sugar has it covered. And you might as well resign yourself to a long night here."

She pleaded up at him with her eyes, really not wanting any fuss.

He put his arm around her and soothed, "Enjoy the company of what Mandy calls made-family. Would Debra throw you an impromptu engagement party?"

She sighed and forced a smile.

He squeezed her. "Trust me after the first glass of wine works on your bones, you'll start having fun."

"Is that right? You expecting fun out of me tonight?" she teased, straight-faced.

He grinned and removed his arm. "You'd be surprised what I expect of you."

Sephie's eyes widened in shock, and the whole table

laughed. She'd almost forgotten they were within earshot, though Mandy was on her left and Laura on Floyd's right. B.D. and James faced them.

Soon, though B.D. and James broke off into a separate conversation, with James studying the picture on B.D.'s phone and asking then about the song he'd sung.

"It's a John Prine song if I remember," B.D. said. "He wrote a lot of songs about life: lonely old couples, drug addicted veterans, depression. 'Angel from Montgomery' is one of his best."

"He wrote that? I thought it was a Bonnie Raitt tune."

"A cover. Is blues your only interest?"

"Pretty much. But I've been doing a lot of church music and even some theater music the Methodist church I played at wanted."

B.D. grinned.

"There's a song I want you to learn," Sephie said. "James has the music."

"What one, Miz Sephie?" the guitarist asked.

"'You Lift Me Up.' You know it?"

"I've heard it, but I never learned it," B.D. admitted.

"Then it's a project for you both."

Just then, Bill appeared again with a tray of filled champagne flutes. As he placed them on the table, he kept glancing around, checking on four servers and the bartender passing out plastic champagne flutes. When they were finished, he called Sugar and the kitchen staff out of the kitchen. Each had a filled plastic flute.

Banging his own glass flute with Mandy's knife, he called for attention. To Sephie and Floyd, he said. "Would you please stand."

They complied though Sephie's face was reddening.

To his patrons, he said, "Raise you glasses for a toast to good friends of mine who are celebrating their engagement. They've both lived long lives with other spouses who have since passed. They found each other here in our fair city and are planning on spending their sunset years together. To Sephie and Floyd, may you have many happy years together!"

Everyone drank and then cheered as Sephie and Floyd sat down. Floyd urged Sephie to enjoy her champagne as he took a sip from his and placed it in front of her. "It's quite good."

Salads soon came out from the kitchen with a condiment tray of salad dressings. Plates with little loaves of bread and two bowls with individually wrapped pats of butter followed. Bill, who was still hovering, said, "We did a big wedding rehearsal and wedding dinner here last week. I think we've got this down." Giving Sephie and Floyd pats on the back, he strolled back to the kitchen.

Picking up her aunt's left hand, Mandy said, "What's this? You didn't go and to the deed already, did you?"

Sephie's face reddened, glancing at Floyd, who was chuckling while pouring Ranch dressing over his lettuce.

"I mean, you didn't already get married by a justice or something, did you?"

Realizing Mandy was talking about the wedding ring she wore, Sephie said, "No, Floyd made me wear my old ring because the church biddies were looking at me funny at the visitation so he thought appearing with him at the funeral with a ring would shut them up."

"I hope it did," Mandy said.

"You have to get her a proper ring," Laura chided Floyd.

"Tomorrow," Floyd said reaching for the bread.

Turning to Sephie, Laura continued, "So, you packed up and put your house on the market."

"It's already sold," Floyd said once he'd swallowed a bite of bread. He looked up and raised a hand at a passing server. "Could you bring me an iced tea please?"

"Sold!" Laura exclaimed. "Already?"

"It wasn't even listed yet," Sephie said. "We've got a contract and need your lawyer to look it over tomorrow."

"I'll call him first thing in the morning," Mandy said. "I'll make sure he squeezes you in."

"Did you get your asking price?" Laura asked innocently.

Sephie choked on the blue cheese drenched lettuce she was trying to eat. Coughing, she reached for the champagne and downed probably more than she should have.

After Sephie recovered, Floyd merely said, "And then some."

"I'd have been happy with just the plain market listing price, which was way too much."

"Sounds like you got a good deal. Anytime you can sell before a house gets listed is good," Laura said.

"Would it be too rude to ask how much?" Mandy said meekly.

Sephie paid attention to her salad but eyed Floyd and nodded.

"Got a piece of paper and a pen?" he asked.

Laura reached into her handbag and pulled out a small note pad and a pen.

Floyd scrawled a figure on the paper while Laura looked on, her face expressing shock, and then he handed it to Mandy.

She read it. Her face looked even more shocked as she sought Laura's. "No way!"

Sephie snatched it away and crumpled it. "A developer is buying. Obviously, he's had his eye on my property for a while."

"Maybe after reading Aunt Agnesia's obituary, I bet," Mandy suggested. "So, that's why you need a good lawyer and financial advisor."

"I shouldn't benefit from what will be done to my mountain."

"A developer? Like in condos and resorts?"

Sephie nodded. "But what can I do? He'd get it no matter who I sold it to. I don't know what to do."

"Aunt Sephie," Laura said slowly. "You could do a lot

of good with that money. Set up a scholarship or a fund for families in need or any number of things to help."

Sephie stopped eating, as ideas began to fill her head. She looked at Mandy and thought about helping with the mortgages on the shop and little house. Her attention turned to B.D. and thought about him entering the university here in a brand-new Master's program combining music and folklore and wondered how he could work, study, and still perform. Her eyes moved to James and wondered how many young musicians were on the Fort Berthold reservation just like him and whether there could be a scholarship for indigenous musicians. She remembered how he and Corinna had gotten along and wondered if there could be a grant program to teach traditional healing on the reservation and others here in North Dakota that might also preserve native languages.

Those thoughts were interrupted as a server put a plate of prime rib, garlic mashed potatoes, and asparagus in front of her and Floyd. Other servers made sure the rest of the party had theirs as well.

"Prime rib?" B.D. said, unbelieving. He waved Bill over. "Weren't you cooking this for a luncheon meeting tomorrow? You were going to finish it off to order then."

He shrugged. "Guess we'll just put another one in the oven."

When Bill had left, B.D. leaned over the table and said conspiratorially. "This was meant for the mayor tomorrow."

James chuckled. "His loss," he said, looking at his meal. Then reverently he added, "'Where paradise lay,'" looking up at each of the faces at the table.

B.D. nodded as the others paused to recall the words from the coal mining song he had sung.

Floyd raised his glass of iced tea. "Amen."

Servers filled beverage orders as they stuffed themselves. James and B.D. made plans to share some songs tomorrow. Laura and Mandy offered wedding suggestions. Sephie and

Floyd merely ate and smiled.

When they were mostly finished with their dinners, Floyd got up and found Bill at the back near the kitchen. The old man reached for his wallet, and Bill wrestled his hand away. There was a lot of head shaking and muffled argument. Sugar emerged from the kitchen with a white bakery box when it looked like the argument might get too heated. She handed it to Floyd. Finally, the old man smiled and said something. Sugar hugged him and Bill shook his hand.

Returning with the box, Floyd announced, "It looks like we have cake for breakfast tomorrow."

"Or tonight," B.D. said.

Placing a hand on B.D.'s shoulder, Floyd said, "For such a tall stringy kid, you have a large capacity for packing away food. Yes, you can have a piece. But we'd like to look at it before you and James over there launch a frontal assault on a defenseless cake."

Their trek back to the shop and the little house was leisurely, full from their meal and content with good company. After B.D. had fetched their bags and put them in their room, Sephie and Floyd paused behind their closed bedroom door. The old man took Sephie into his arms.

"If you're expecting fun out of me after that heavy meal, you can just dream on," Sephie protested, trying to suppress a smile.

He merely shook his head and said, "James was right. This is where paradise is." He then kissed the old woman soundly.

The End

About the Author

Janie Franz comes from a long line of liars and storytellers with roots deep in east Tennessee and honed by the frigid winters of the Northern Plains and the ever-changing landscape of the high desert and mountains of New Mexico. She is an author, a professional speaker, and reviewer. Previously, she ran her own online music publication (Refrain Magazine) and was an agent/publicist for a groove/funk band, a radio announcer, and a yoga/relaxation instructor. Readers' comments welcome at janie@janiefranzauthor.com